MAYA'S SECRET

♥

HOLLY WEBB

nosy
crow

First published 2014 by Nosy Crow Ltd
The Crow's Nest, 10a Lant Street
London SE1 1QR
www.nosycrow.com

ISBN: 978 0 85763 105 3

Nosy Crow and associated logos are trademarks
and/or registered trademarks of Nosy Crow Ltd

Text © Holly Webb 2014
Cover and inside pattern © Hannah Chapman 2014

The right of Holly Webb to be identified as the author has been asserted.

A CIP catalogue record for this book is available from the British Library.

Printed and bound in the UK by Clays Ltd, St Ives Plc.
Typeset by Tiger Media Ltd, Bishops Stortford, Hertfordshire

Papers used by Nosy Crow are made from wood grown in

MAYA'S SECRET

Look out for more stories
about MAYA and her friends:

IZZY'S
RIVER

♥

POPPY'S
GARDEN

♥

EMILY'S
DREAM

ONE

Maya slipped into the classroom, hoping no one would notice her. She was halfway to the table she shared with Poppy and Emily, when Mr Finlay turned round from the whiteboard. Maya sighed. She hadn't even missed numeracy.

"Hello, Maya!" He looked confused for a moment. "Are you all right? Oh, your mum sent a note, didn't she? Something about…" He trailed off, catching the panicked look on Maya's face. "Um. Yes. An appointment. Right, go and sit down, please."

Maya hurried to their table, her cheeks burning.

Emily leaned over. "Where have you been?"

"Doctor's." Maya crossed her fingers under the table. There was no way she was telling them the truth. She'd never live it down.

"What's wrong with you?" Emily asked, eyeing her doubtfully.

1

"Nothing, just a cold. Mum was fussing." Maya scrabbled around for her pencil case so she could avoid looking at Poppy and Emily. She wished they'd stop asking questions. She hated lying to her friends.

"Actually, you do look really red round the eyes," Poppy told her. "Maybe you're getting a cold. I'll bring you in some throat pastilles I made, they're excellent."

Maya smiled nervously. She'd had experience of Poppy's homemade remedies before. Her friend was really into natural cures – like putting spiders' webs on cuts to heal them. A couple of weeks ago, when Maya had tripped in the playground, Poppy had disappeared off on a spider-hunting expedition and made Mr Finlay panic that she'd run away to join the circus. (Not all that unlikely.) Luckily she hadn't found any. It wasn't that Maya was scared of spiders, just that she hated the thought of their claggy webs on her skin, even though Poppy swore to her that it was safe. "*And* cobwebs are bio-degradable, Maya," she'd promised, knowing how much her friend worried about the mountains of landfill all over the place. "Not like plasters. They've been used on wounds since the Middle Ages, honestly."

2

Maya still wasn't convinced. Didn't people always die really young in the Middle Ages? It was probably because of all the spiders' webs.

Anyway, there was no way she was even trying the throat sweets – who knew what Poppy had put in them? Chocolate and nettles or something. She'd have to flush them down the loo. But she didn't want to hurt Poppy's feelings. "OK," she murmured, crossing her fingers under the table again. Emily rolled her eyes at her, just a little.

Anyway, Maya didn't really have a cold. The red eyes probably just meant she was allergic to the stupid false eyelashes Mum's stylist had insisted she wore for the magazine photoshoot.

It was worth it, though. The interviewer had let Maya talk about cruelty-free make-up, and she'd promised they'd put that bit in the article. Mum had even said she liked to use animal-friendly brands too, after Maya had elbowed her in the ribs to remind her they had a deal. She'd refused to do the last two photoshoots, so Mum would have promised her almost anything.

No one she knew was ever going to see it, anyway, Maya told herself hopefully. No one at this school seemed to read celeb magazines much. Anyway, with

that much make-up on, the photos wouldn't even look like her…

It would have been different if she'd still been at Graham House, her old school. There all the girls would have been passing the magazine around. Someone would have recognised India Kell, and they would have gone on and on about it for days, as though it was the most exciting thing in the world that Maya's mum used to be a singer.

She still was, Maya supposed. But her mum mostly did TV presenting now. People always wanted to interview her. The magazines wanted to talk about her clothes, and her house, and her favourite make-up. And Maya. Her mum had a book of all the photo spreads from over the years – Maya as a baby, Maya the cute toddler, all the way up to age seven when she'd stopped enjoying it. She wanted to wear scruffy old jeans, not dress up and put on lipgloss so her mum could show her off.

Maya tried to listen to what Mr Finlay was talking about, but her thoughts kept taking over. It would be OK; it wasn't as if she had the same surname as her mum – she was Maya Knight, and no one would expect to find boring Maya Knight in a celeb magazine. She'd worked hard at being boring, ever since she came to Park Road School.

When Maya had begged her parents to let her move schools, they'd been really shocked – she'd been going to Graham House since nursery. It was the only school she'd known, everyone knew her too, and all her friends were there. It was even one of the reasons her parents had moved close to Millford in the first place. How could she want to leave?

"Maya, is someone bullying you?" her dad had asked anxiously, leaning over the table to grab her hands. They were in a restaurant, a smart one that had just opened somewhere in London. Maya couldn't remember where. It was her dad's birthday.

Maya's eyelashes fluttered now as she thought about him, her lovely dad. He'd been so worried about her. He knew she wasn't happy at Graham House, but he hated having to go into the school. He said the head teacher always made him feel stupid. She'd watched him across the table that night, swallowing nervously as he thought about it. It was funny that someone who wrote such amazing songs couldn't find the right words when he was talking to a teacher.

"No. I'm fine." Maya had stared at them both, widening her eyes as though it would make her look

5

more truthful. She really wanted them to believe her – and not just to believe, but to understand how she felt. "No one's mean to me, ever. Because I might invite them over, Mum, and they'd get to meet you. They could say they've hung out with India Kell." She'd frowned, kicking at the table leg. Someone on the other side of the room had recognised her mum, she could see them whispering, and doing that funny ducking up and down people did when they were trying to stare without being obvious. It never worked. She looked up and glared back at the woman, who went pink and pretended she was just talking to her friend. Maya felt guilty, but only a little bit.

"I don't believe that's true, Maya." Her mum's eyes were widening too – that was where she'd got the look from, Maya suddenly realised. It was the way her mum looked when she sang, whenever she was really deep in the song. Her eyes were a dark, purplish blue, like Maya's. "You've got such good friends there. You've known Macey since you were three, come on!"

Maya nodded reluctantly. OK, her mum was right. She would miss Macey. But there was no way that she was going to lose touch with her. Macey was her best friend, and the only person at Graham House who'd ever dared say anything that wasn't wonderful about Maya's mum. Everyone else had been going on about how brilliant her last album was, and Macey had asked Maya if she really liked it. Maya didn't listen to her mum's music that much. It was too weird, especially the songs that were about her. So she'd only shrugged, and Macey nodded. "Mmm. I could take it or leave it, I suppose."

No one ever said anything like that.

"Macey can come and stay in the holidays," Maya had pointed out that night. "Or I could go and stay with her. I'd miss her loads, of course I would, but not any of the others."

Her mum was shaking her head. "I don't see how it would work, Maya. Schools like Graham House understand how to look after celebrity children."

Maya made a face. "I'm not a celebrity," she muttered. "I don't want to be. That's why I want to change schools!"

"Most girls would love all the attention you get." Her mum was staring at the pattern woven into the tablecloth, and her purplish eyes were all shiny with tears now too. Maya pulled her hands back from her dad, and sat on them. She was *not* going to give up

and go and hug her mum, and say it was all OK. It wasn't.

"Everything shouldn't be about whose daughter I am!"

"You sound like you wish you belonged to somebody else!" Her mum was trying to laugh, but her voice was really hurt, and Maya sighed miserably.

"Of course I don't. I just want to be me. Not India Kell's daughter. And I can't do that unless I go to a different school."

"But Maya, you *are* a celebrity child, and the local primary school isn't going to be able to deal with all that." Her mum sat up straight, sounding decided, but her dad was folding his napkin into a strange flower shape, and frowning.

"Would it really be that difficult?" he asked. "We'd have to explain to the school, I suppose. Ask them to be understanding."

"Why?" Maya muttered. She hadn't wanted anyone making a fuss. But her dad had been right – it wasn't fair to expect Park Road School not to ask questions when, after another three weeks of begging, she turned up two weeks into Year Six. And her mum never went to Parents' Evening, or the school play. Her dad came instead, with sunglasses on. People didn't recognise him very much. He'd suggested a hat and a big scarf as well; Maya suspected he liked being undercover. He wanted to be boring too, sometimes.

Maya frowned down at her work. Boring was the wrong word. Normal. She just wanted to be normal, like Poppy and Emily.

She stifled a laugh, stuffing the back of her fist into her mouth and feeling suddenly better. Even though she was still worrying about the magazine spread, she couldn't help it. Poppy the spider-web queen, normal?

Her friend was leaning over the maths worksheet that Mr Finlay had handed out, and her wavy browny-blonde hair was swinging forward and falling out of its ponytail. Maya could see the blue and green streaks underneath. Poppy loved dying her hair, but they weren't supposed to for school, so she only streaked the under layers. She'd explained to them that the blue meant the sea and the sky, and the green was the earth. Poppy was just waiting for her next allowance so she could get a fiery red dye too. Maya couldn't quite remember what the red meant – probably volcanoes. Or life force, or something like that. Sometimes Maya suspected Poppy was making it up as she went along, but she could be so funny

about it, no one minded.

Emily nudged Poppy and pointed at her hair, nodding at Mr Finlay, who was walking round checking their work. Mr Finlay might not notice dyed hair, but their classroom assistant Miss Grace was wandering around too, and she definitely would. Poppy stared at Emily vaguely, and then seemed to wake up, hurriedly tucking her hair behind her ears to hide the coloured streaks, and beaming gratefully.

"We'll go on with those worksheets tomorrow," Mr Finlay called over the sudden scraping of chairs as the bell rang for lunch. "I've got something exciting for you all this afternoon!"

Emily whispered in Maya's ear. "More maps!"

Maya snorted with laughter. Mr Finlay loved maps; he kept bringing them in and spreading them out over all the tables. They'd measured bits of maps for numeracy, drawn their own maps in art lessons, and the maps were always coming out in literacy so they could be inspired by the names of the places scattered all over them. Poppy was convinced Mr Finlay had a map tattooed all over his back; she swore she'd seen it through his shirt once. Maya wouldn't have been surprised. She'd really enjoyed writing a mad story about smugglers, when her table had been given an old map of Cornwall a few weeks back. But everyone in 6F was getting a bit sick of maps now. All the boys did was try and find rude place names – Strawberry Bottom had got Nick Drayton sent to Mrs Angel's office for the whole of lunch.

"Are you feeling better?" Poppy asked, draping an arm round Maya's shoulders, and peering at her anxiously.

"You have to hope she is or you'll have caught her lurgy, hugging her like that," Emily pointed out.

Poppy shook her head calmly. "No. I won't catch anything."

Emily folded her arms. "Are you wearing that crystal necklace again? I thought Mrs Angel made you take it off?"

Poppy sighed. "No. She still wasn't being fair, though. It wasn't jewellery. It was protection. And by the time she gave it back to me it wasn't working any more. She'd been keeping it in a drawer, and that one really needed sunlight."

"You could put it under a sunbed, you know, really charge it up again." Emily giggled.

Poppy sucked in a horrified breath. "Fake sunlight? It'd probably poison me if I wore it after that!"

"Sunbeds kill people," Maya put in, and Emily

laughed at her.

"They do! UV rays are really bad for you."

"I know they are, but it was the way you said it. Like this mean sunbed was going to creep up on Poppy, and squash her to death. Evil sunbeds. They're coming to get you!"

Maya scowled, but Emily elbowed her, grinning. "Don't be so grumpy! It was funny!" She made claws of her fingers, scrunched her nose and showed all her teeth. It was amazing how ugly somebody so pretty could look all of a sudden. "Grrrr! I am an evil sunbed…"

The corner of Maya's mouth quirked up just a smidge, and then she grinned back. "Oh, all right. I suppose it was a *bit* funny. Only a bit, though. Poppy, what are you using to not get ill then, if the crystal's broken?"

"Herb tea. I've got some in a flask in my lunch box, you can try it if you like."

Maya gave her a surprised look. Herbal tea was surprisingly normal for Poppy. Her dad drank herbal tea all the time, he said coffee kept him awake too much. "Does that stop you being ill?" She'd have to tell Dad.

"My kind does. I made it myself. It's got mint and

dandelions in it. And golden syrup."

"Dandelions are weeds, Poppy." Emily was eyeing her friend worriedly. "Are you really eating them?"

"No, you chop them up and pour hot water over them. The leaves as well. It's very good for you. I got it out of a book from the library on nature's secret remedies."

"Do those books call out to you when you go in the library?" Emily shook her head. "You've always got some random book under your bed. Is the tea nice?"

Poppy went pink. "Actually, it tastes horrible," she admitted. "That's why I put the golden syrup in it. It's not in the recipe, but it sort of hides the taste of the dandelions. Almost."

"You're really selling it, Poppy…" Maya told her. "I'll pass."

"It works though!" Poppy protested. "I haven't been ill for ages. Well. Since Tuesday, when I found the recipe."

"Four whole days. It's a miracle." Emily nodded solemnly. Then she sighed. "Who knows what's in *my* lunch. I'll be lucky if it's not a pot of mashed-up carrot and banana, or something else disgusting. I can't stand bananas, but Mum's trying all kinds of random stuff to get Sukie to eat. She's the world's

fussiest baby. I think I'll make my own sandwiches tomorrow."

"Oooh, banana sandwiches… I might ask Anna to do me some of those." Maya was suddenly hungry. "Come on, let's go and eat lunch." Because her mum and dad were quite often out of the country they had a housekeeper who looked after Maya a lot of the time. But Maya never called her that in front of anyone at school. It sounded far too posh. Too pop-starry, having "staff". But Anna picked her up from school occasionally, if she was in town or Maya needed school uniform or something. Emily had thought Anna was Maya's mum, so she'd had to explain. She'd told Emily that Anna was her au pair. It didn't sound quite as show-offish. But even then Emily had raised her eyebrows. "An au pair?"

"Yeah, because my mum works," Maya muttered.

Emily nodded. "I s'pose. My mum would kill for an au pair. Is she nice?"

Anna was, very. But she usually made Maya's lunches for her, and she disapproved of Maya being a vegetarian. She was from Spain, and being vegetarian wasn't as common there as it was in Britain. Anna had been known to "accidentally" put ham sandwiches in Maya's lunch box, in

14

the hope that she might be tempted. She thought Maya was going to waste away without eating any meat, even though Maya had explained to her loads of times that humans were better off eating mostly vegetables anyway. Anna always just sniffed. Whenever she and Maya argued about it, she'd cook roast chicken for dinner the next day. She knew it was the hardest thing for Maya to resist. Veggie sausages just didn't cut it next to roast potatoes and gravy, especially with those bits of spicy sausage she added. Maya's mouth was watering just thinking about it, and it was cheese sandwiches for lunch – again.

The girls found a free table in the hall and got out their lunches. Emily and Maya watched Poppy opening up her flask. She poured out a cupful of dull, greenish liquid, with bits in.

"Forget sunbeds, *that* looks poisonous." Emily shuddered. "You're not really going to drink it? Urrggghh, Poppy, don't!"

"It isn't that bad." Poppy swallowed a mouthful, and grimaced. "Not enough golden syrup. I should have put honey in it instead. But Jake and Alex keep using it all up making toast. They just live on toast. Dad says it's because they're teenagers, they need a

lot of energy. But they eat a loaf of bread every day. Each!"

Emily nodded sympathetically. "Brothers... You're so lucky not having any, Maya. I would love to be the only one."

"Wouldn't you miss them?" Maya asked doubtfully.

Emily wrinkled her nose. "I might miss Sukie. When she's not yelling, anyway. But Toby and James are just..." She shrugged. "Well, you know what they're like."

Maya smiled. She'd never met Jake and Alex, Poppy's twin brothers; they were at secondary school, and the one time she'd been to Poppy's house, they'd been holed up in their room, their music making the kitchen ceiling tremble. She had noticed a large pile of crumbs and a couple of sticky knives by the toaster, though, now she thought about it. But everyone at Park Road knew Toby and James, Emily's little brothers. James was only in Reception, but he followed Toby around like he was tied on, and the pair of them were in the middle of every pile-up in the playground. If something got broken, they would be there, looking very sweetly sorry.

"What's really unfair is they get away with it because they're cute," Emily muttered. "Mum wants to put wings on them and Sukie and take a photo of them all to be our family Christmas card. With tinsel round their heads."

Maya nearly choked on her sandwich. Toby and James looked a lot like Emily, with dark curly hair and chocolate-dark eyes. They would look gorgeous in haloes. But anyone who knew them would see through the angelic looks. "Seriously?"

Emily nodded. "She doesn't think they're naughty at all. Whenever anyone mentions it at school, she thinks they're just making a fuss. And she says I ought to look out for them at school! I don't need to look out for *them*, they beat me up in the playground!" She unwrapped her sandwiches. "Look! Tuna, and I hate it. But Toby wanted tuna in his, and Mum's used up the rest of the tin on mine. Ugh."

"Do you want a cheese one? Anna did me loads. She thinks if there's no ham or anything like that, then I have to have twice as much of everything else to make up for it." Maya handed over a cheese sandwich, and Emily bit into it gratefully.

"You're a star. Sure you don't want a tuna one back? You don't ever have fish either?"

Maya shook her head. "No, it's OK." She'd been fishing once, on a boat in America somewhere, with

some people from Mum's record company. The fish had been huge – great silvery things called marlin, with spiky noses. Dad had loved it, but Maya had seen the fish struggling and fighting against the lines and it made her feel sick – sicker, anyway; the rocking of the boat was already doing bad things to her insides. She could see the fish's eyes, and it seemed to be looking at her. It wasn't like it was cute, or furry. Actually, it looked a bit mean. But she still didn't want anybody to kill it.

"I'm binning them, then," Emily muttered. "And don't tell me it's a terrible waste, Maya, because I already know, and I'm still not eating them. Thank you, Toby."

Maya nibbled the edge of her sandwich thoughtfully. She was lucky having Mum and Dad all to herself when they were home. No brothers nicking the nice things out of the cupboards, or getting her in trouble at school. No baby sister taking up all their time. But it would be nice to have someone else to hang around with, especially when her parents were away so much. Mum kept saying to invite her friends from school round, but Maya wasn't sure. Their house was pretty big, and it was full of photos and things. If Poppy and Emily came round, she was sure they'd be able to work out who her mum was, even if they didn't actually meet her. And that was exactly what she'd moved schools to get away from.

TWO

"It's going to be another map thing. I bet you – umm – the rest of the packet of Polos in my rucksack." Emily folded her arms, and waited for Mr Finlay to prove her right.

Maya shook her head. "I don't know. I can't see any maps lying around. Oooh!"

Mr Finlay had been rummaging in his bag, and now he held up a large bar of chocolate. Everyone had been feeling sleepy after lunch, but now the class brightened up at once. If this project involved chocolate, they liked it.

"Polos, please!" Maya hissed at Emily.

"Hold on." Emily flapped a hand at her. "We could be making maps of chocolate-growing jungles." But she sounded doubtful.

Poppy smiled dreamily. "A whole forest of toffee trees…" She started to draw in her notebooks, sketching lollipop forests, with little sweetie birds flying through them, until Emily elbowed her in the ribs. Poppy was always getting into trouble for doodling. Mr Finlay said it meant she wasn't listening and he didn't believe her when she promised him that it actually helped her listen better. He refused to test it out, either, like Emily suggested, which all three of them agreed was totally unfair.

"Who can tell me what's important about this chocolate?" Mr Finlay asked, waving it dramatically at the class.

"It's milk chocolate?" Lucy, who sat on the next table to Maya and the others, asked.

Mr Finlay shook his head. "Someone else?"

"There's not enough of it for all of us?" one of the boys called out. "Do we have to win it?"

"The person who gets the answer right gets the first piece, and I've got another bar as well. You'll all get some, don't worry," Mr Finlay promised. "Look at it carefully."

Maya peered at the wrapping. She recognised that little blue and green logo. She waved her hand hopefully. "Is it Fairtrade chocolate?"

"Exactly!" Mr Finlay tore the packet open, and handed her a few squares. "Share that round your

table. Fairtrade chocolate. Maya, can you tell us what it means, as well?"

Maya tucked the square of chocolate into her cheek with her tongue, and nodded. "The people who picked the cocoa beans got paid properly," she said, in a chocolate-muffled voice.

"And they don't make children work," Emily added. "The money from the chocolate helps pay for them to go to school."

"I'd rather make chocolate than go to school any day," Nick said, smirking.

Mr Finlay looked at him thoughtfully, then turned round to the white board, and put up a photo of a boy who looked about their age. He was wearing a ragged T-shirt and shorts, and he was grinning at the camera – even though he was lugging a sack on his shoulders that looked half as big as he was. Mr Finlay clicked through a series of photos – trees, with children standing under them holding baskets, then another little boy who looked about seven, holding a massive knife, longer than his arm. In the next picture, the same boy was sitting next to a huge pile of greenish-red pods, the size of melons.

"What are those?" Poppy asked, frowning. They didn't look like anything to do with chocolate.

"Cocoa pods." Mr Finlay pointed to the one the boy was splitting open with his enormous knife. "You have to break them open with a machete to get the cocoa beans out. Cocoa beans are what chocolate is made from."

"And children do that?" Emily asked doubtfully. It didn't look very safe. That boy was the same age as Toby. "Imagine Toby with one of those!" she hissed to Maya.

Maya nodded, and pulled a face. It didn't bear thinking about.

Mr Finlay went on to the next photo – the same boy, but with a group of people that had to be his family, standing in front of a wobbly-looking house with a metal roof. "They don't have a lot of choice. Most of the cocoa beans that we get our chocolate from grow on little farms called groves, and lots of the groves are run by only one family. So when it's harvest time everyone who *can* work has to. Even the children. If they don't harvest the cocoa beans, and sell them on, they don't eat." He smiled at Nick. "Still think it's better than school?"

Nick shrugged one shoulder, looking embarrassed. "It doesn't look all that bad," he muttered.

"A whole day, using a knife on the end of a stick to

cut cocoa pods off trees? Even if you're tired?"

"He's got a bandage round his leg," someone pointed out quietly. Maya glanced round, surprised. Izzy was really mouse-like – she hardly ever said anything in class, even though Mr Finlay was always telling her how good her work was, especially when they did science.

"And it looks all dirty," someone said. "He'll catch something. He ought to get it checked at the hospital."

Mr Finlay nodded. "But I shouldn't think there is one, Leah. Not for a few hundred miles, maybe. And the roads – this is in a place called Ivory Coast, it's the world's biggest cocoa producer – the roads there are all falling apart. It's difficult to get anywhere."

"So, he never goes to school?" Maya asked. The chocolate had left her mouth dry, and she swallowed.

"That's right. These photos are from a news website reporting on children who work. This boy, Sami, he works in his uncle's cocoa grove. Only about half the people in Ivory Coast can read, because they've never been able to go to school. They've always worked, or looked after their families."

Maya looked down at the Fairtrade mark. "But this chocolate – no children made that, did they?"

Mr Finlay was silent for a moment. "No one can

promise that, Maya, to be honest," he said eventually. "Fairtrade works by getting farmers to sign up to a list of things, like paying their workers properly, making sure they're safe, protecting them if they're using dangerous chemicals. And one of the things they agree to is not using child labour. But these families, if they never let children work in the cocoa groves, ever, they wouldn't survive. The children would be worse off than if they *were* working because they'd have no money for food. There's a difference between child labour that treats children really badly, and helping on the farm when your family needs you. So the answer is that children probably did help make this chocolate, Maya. But the Fairtrade organisation paid more money to their parents for the cocoa beans, so the parents could afford to send them to school when it wasn't the busy harvest time. You see what I mean?"

"But children should go to school every day," Emily muttered. "If it was here, those parents would be in trouble."

"Cocoa beans grow in really poor countries, though, Emily. School is a luxury. About half the people in Ivory Coast are living in poverty – they've got less than ninety pence a day to live on. That's

25

for buying all their food, oil for cooking, clothes, medicines if they need them. School comes further down the list of priorities. But that's part of what the Fairtrade people do – the Fairtrade chocolate costs more for us to buy, because the extra money gets used for helping the people who produce the cocoa. They work with charities in places like Ivory Coast to build schools, and health clinics, so Sami could get someone to look at his leg."

"Do they ever get to eat the chocolate?" Poppy asked suddenly, and then looked at the table as everyone stared at her. "I just wondered. They work so hard for it," she murmured.

"No, it's a good question, Poppy." Mr Finlay frowned. "I don't know."

Maya licked a smudge of chocolate off her thumb. It was very sweet. "I bet they don't. There's a chocolate factory not far from here, isn't there? Probably most of the cocoa beans get made into chocolate in factories in other countries."

"Perhaps you can find that out, Poppy." Mr Finlay held up the chocolate wrapper again. "This is going to be our new project, for the next few weeks. I want you to work in small groups, and create some sort of display on Fairtrade."

"Fairtrade chocolate?" Maya asked. "Or just Fairtrade anything?"

"Anything to do with Fairtrade. Who can tell me something else that you can buy with a Fairtrade mark?"

"Bananas!"

"Sugar?" Poppy asked. "I think we've got some sugar that's Fairtrade." She frowned. "But the golden syrup isn't," she added to Maya and Emily in a whisper. "I might have to change my tea recipe. I can't believe those pictures. Those boys were younger than us."

"I know. Loads of the stuff in our cupboards isn't Fairtrade," Emily whispered back, shaking her head. "I can't see Mum agreeing to buy Fairtrade everything though, it's really expensive. A bit would help, wouldn't it?" she asked hopefully.

"Of course it would." Maya leaned her chin on her hands and sighed. "I love chocolate. Anna buys the Fairtrade kind for cooking, but chocolate buttons aren't Fairtrade. I'd miss them."

"I want you to try and be really imaginative," Mr Finlay called, over the buzz of everyone arguing about who they wanted to work with. "Not just a list of facts. Something exciting! And there will be a

prize for the best projects!"

"Will it be more chocolate?" Nick asked hopefully, but Mr Finlay only gave a secretive smile.

"Perhaps we could do a taste test on Fairtrade chocolate." Emily smiled blissfully. "A really careful one. You know, giving them all stars. And flavour notes... *Hints of vanilla and lemon...* We could compare them to not-Fairtrade chocolate too."

"I take it you three are working together then?" Mr Finlay asked, making a note on the list he was carrying around.

Maya blinked. They hadn't even thought about it, just started talking about what they'd do. "Yes, please," she agreed, and Poppy and Emily just nodded, as though it was a bit of a silly question.

"Do you think we could do some cooking as part of the project?" Poppy asked, and Mr Finlay was thinking about it when Izzy came and stood beside him. She looked pink and embarrassed, Maya thought, glancing away quickly.

Izzy reminded her too much of how she'd felt when she moved to Park Road. Maya had been lucky that Mr Finlay had given her Emily as a mentor, and she'd got on really well with her and Poppy, even from the first day. But for the first few weeks she'd not quite known if that was only because Emily *had* to be nice to her. She did a lot of hanging around, wondering if she was allowed to say anything. Poppy and Emily had been friends since Reception, and it wasn't even as if Maya had arrived on the first day of Year Six, when everyone was getting used to each other again after the holidays. She felt like she was always a bit in the way, or doing the wrong thing.

The feeling faded after a couple of weeks, especially after Emily invited her over. You didn't have to have people you'd only been told to like over for tea, did you?

"Mr Finlay…" Izzy muttered. "Do we have to work in a group? Can I do my project on my own, please?"

Maya looked up again sharply.

Mr Finlay sucked in a breath. "Well, I don't think so, Izzy, sorry. Part of the point of the project is that you work together. A team."

Izzy nodded, and darted a look around the classroom. Everyone else was huddled in groups, or at least twos, mostly talking about chocolate.

"Don't worry!" Mr Finlay sounded determinedly cheerful. "We'll find you a group to join."

Izzy stared at her shoes.

She's crying, Maya realised in horror. *Eeek. I would be too. Imagine having to go and beg to be in someone's group. She'll probably end up with Lucy and Ali and that lot, and they'll make her do all the work, and be really mean to her.*

"Izzy, do you want to be in our group?" she asked, before she could think too much about it.

Poppy, Emily and Izzy all looked at her in complete shock, until Maya kicked Poppy under the table. Only gently.

Poppy jumped, and then said, "Um. Yes. Come with us."

"That's very nice of you, girls." Mr Finlay beamed. "I'll think about the cooking, Poppy." And he hurried off to sort out an argument on the other side of the classroom.

"What did you do that for?" Emily hissed in Maya's ear, as Izzy went to fetch her stuff. "We don't want her, she's so boring!"

"I don't think she is." Poppy looked thoughtfully over at Izzy, who was stuffing things into her pencil case slowly, with her hair hanging over her face so no one could see her red eyes. "She just doesn't talk a lot, that's all. Sometimes she's quite funny. Especially in PE."

Emily sighed. "I wanted it to be just us doing our

project. You could have come round to mine so we could work on it. I don't want to invite Izzy too! I don't like her!"

"Why not?" Maya looked at her in surprise. Izzy was so quiet it was hard to think of there being anything about her to dislike.

Emily scowled. "Toby kicked a football at her in the playground last year. It was an accident," she added hastily. "But she was really nasty to him."

"He broke her glasses!" Poppy pointed out. "And *you're* nasty to him all the time."

"Yeah, but he's my brother, I'm allowed. It's different!" Emily muttered. "And I don't like her anyway. She's stuck-up. She thinks she's better than everyone else. Goes round with her nose in the air the whole time."

Maya looked at Izzy, who was still slowly gathering her things, as though she knew they were talking about her. She didn't look stuck-up. At all. But she was so, so shy. She hardly ever talked to anyone. Maybe that's why Emily thought she was snotty?

"Sorry," Maya muttered. "She looked really sad. I only wanted to cheer her up."

Emily sighed. "Your problem is that you're too nice. It's probably because you haven't got any brothers."

Izzy was threading her way back between the tables, and now she stood in front of them, clutching her pencil case and trying to look as if she didn't care what they said. "You don't have to let me be in your group if you don't want to. I can do it on my own."

She looked even more like a mouse with red eyes, Maya thought. A little white mouse, with that whitish-blonde hair, and her pale eyelashes.

"No, you can't," she pointed out, shrugging. "He'll make you go and sit on Ali's table. Or with Ryan and George." She knew that Ali picked on Izzy all the time, and the boys teased her, nicking her book off her when she was sitting reading at lunchtime.

Izzy shot a quick look behind her at the group of boys, who were spitting bits of screwed up chocolate wrapper at each other. "All right. Thank you," she added, not that she really sounded as if she meant it. She sat down, a bit sulkily, and dumped her pencil case on the table.

"Anyway, Mr Finlay's always going on about how brilliant your work is," Maya added. "Our project will be better if you're working on it, too. And it means you don't have to do the whole project by yourself, and make Ryan and the others write one stupid sentence each, and then have everyone telling

32

them how well they've done."

Izzy smiled reluctantly. "When we did those Christmas poems, I wrote the whole thing for George," she admitted. "He just copied his bit out. And he still spelled it all wrong."

Emily wasn't listening. She was leaning backwards, eavesdropping on the table behind them, where Ali, Lucy, Jane and Rachel were sitting. Then she tipped herself up straight again, the chair legs hitting the floor with a thud, and glared. "They heard!" she told the others in a hissy whisper. "They've nicked our idea, about the taste test. They're going to write it all up in a table, like a science experiment." She scowled at Izzy, as though it was somehow her fault, as she was the one who liked science.

"We could still do it," Maya said, but Emily was right. The fun had gone out of it if someone else was going to do the same. Mr Finlay had said to be imaginative.

They sat silently for a moment, listening to everyone else planning excitedly, and Maya felt guilty. Maybe she *had* spoiled everything by letting Izzy join their group.

"Everyone's doing their project on chocolate," Izzy said, after a minute or so.

"Of course they are!" Emily snapped at her. "We're supposed to."

Izzy shrank back in her chair a little, and Maya winced. This was going to be a disaster.

But Poppy leaned forward, shooting Emily a quick look. "No, Mr Finlay said anything to do with Fairtrade. We could do a project on bananas instead. Then that would be different from everyone else."

"I hate bananas," Emily said grumpily.

"But Izzy's right." Poppy looked at Emily sternly. "Everyone's doing chocolate, so let's be different. It doesn't have to be bananas. I bet we could find something else. Sugar, we said, didn't we?"

Maya shook her head, noticing that Izzy had gone pink again, but this time because she was pleased. "I don't know. A project about sugar doesn't sound very exciting."

"That's because nothing's as exciting as chocolate." Poppy sighed. "I'll go home and look at what Mum's got in the kitchen. She gets lots of Fairtrade stuff."

"I suppose bananas would be all right if we can't find anything else. I don't have to actually *eat* the bananas, just write about them," Emily said, but her voice was so gloomy that everyone laughed, even Izzy.

MAYA'S SECRET

"You all need to go and change for PE in a minute, so just a couple of things to remember. This project is going to be most of your homework for the next couple of weeks," Mr Finlay explained. "And there'll be time to work on it in class. But for tonight, please try and start doing some research at home."

"We'd better decide what we want the project to be about then," Izzy pointed out. She sounded almost enthusiastic. "We can't do research if we don't know what we're researching."

Mr Finlay heard her, and looked pleased. "You're doing something else, not chocolate? That's great, girls. Don't worry, Izzy. There'll be plenty of time. Just use tonight for coming up with ideas."

"We'll find something better than bananas," Poppy whispered to Emily.

"Thanks," Emily muttered back. Maya could tell she was feeling guilty about being bad-tempered. Emily was like that – she said mean things, sometimes, and then regretted them minutes after. Maya had got used to it. But she still wasn't even looking at Izzy. The stupid thing was that if she and Emily could get over their spat from last year, Maya had a feeling they'd get on really well. But for that to happen, they were actually going to have to talk to each other…

"I hate PE," Izzy sighed, as they got changed next to each other, and Maya nodded.

"Me too. But maybe we can keep thinking about the project. It'll be athletics again. Loads of waiting around. Maybe we'll have a brilliant idea."

Izzy looked at her sideways, and Maya giggled. "You never know."

THREE

"Are you catching the bus today?" Emily asked Maya as they packed up their stuff after PE.

Maya nodded. "Someone's going to have to pinch me when it's time to get off, I'm so tired after all that running."

Maya and Emily both lived in villages outside Millford, and they usually caught the school bus that wound all round the town dropping people off. It was one of the things Maya liked about Park Road. When she'd been at Graham House, everyone drove to school, and hardly anybody lift-shared. There was always a line of huge cars blocking up the road outside the school, even though half the children were boarding.

She loved the journey in and out of all the little villages, and the extra time she had for chatting with Emily. Quite often in the mornings Maya would see

37

her and Toby and James pelting down the hill, racing the bus to the stop. They were almost always late, and Mr Green, the driver, would moan and threaten to go without them, but he never did. Everyone on the bus would bang on the windows, and cheer when Emily and her brothers finally climbed up the steps. And then Emily's mum would come panting after them, apologise to Mr Green and promise to be on time the next day, and Emily would slump in the seat next to Maya to tell her that Toby had poured two Weetabix and half a pint of milk on James, and then James hadn't got any more clean shirts, so Mum had had to dry him with a hair dryer. There was always something. Maya knew how much Emily got annoyed with her mad family, but it still sounded a lot of fun – more fun than eating breakfast on her own like she usually did, anyway.

Maya smiled to herself. That morning she'd actually had breakfast with her mum and dad – and two make-up artists, a stylist, the photographer, his assistant and the journalist writing the interview. Anna had been in her element; she'd been fussing about it for days, and throwing wobblies because she couldn't get exactly the right sort of flour for her maple syrup pancakes. Maya had eaten so many

practice ones, she was a bit sick of pancakes now.
And it would probably be leftover croissants for tea.
Hopefully all the magazine people would have gone
by the time she got home.

She and Emily managed to get the back seat of the
bus, and Maya slumped down with a sigh.

"Are you still feeling ill?" Emily asked
sympathetically. "You should have got your mum to
give you a note for PE."

Maya looked at her blankly for a second, and
then remembered her excuse from the morning and
crossed her fingers in the folds of her skirt. "No, it's
OK. It isn't a really bad cold. I'm just sleepy."

Emily nodded. "At least we haven't got loads of
homework tonight. I still can't think of anything
brilliant for this project, though. I'll have to go home
and look up Fairtrade stuff on the net like Mr Finlay
said."

Maya was staring thoughtfully out of the window.
"There must be something better than bananas. I
suppose if we did sugar we could do some cooking
like Poppy wanted, but we might have to do that at
home." She frowned at her reflection in the glass.
She'd love to invite Poppy and Emily round to make
stuff at hers. Izzy, too, even. Sooner or later she was

going to have to. It helped that she caught the bus, so it was a bit trickier to arrange things like that. It gave her a good excuse. For her birthday she and her dad had taken Poppy and Emily to the cinema in Millford, and then to Maya's favourite café for tea, instead of having a sleepover or anything like that.

They were trundling through Appleby, the first of the villages on the way home, when the bus stopped in traffic and Maya suddenly leaned forward, rubbing away the mist she'd breathed on to the window. "Emily, look at that new shop."

"Hey, that looks good." Emily leaned over her to see. "Daisy. Cute name. And it's definitely not just stuff for adults. I love that yellow dress."

"I know, it's really nice." But Maya was frowning at the window display, where the clothes were surrounded by enormous flowers and life-size toy dogs with signs round their necks. "Look at those signs. There's a Fairtrade logo on the window! And it says organic, underneath. Do you think it sells food too? Like a café in the back, or something? It doesn't look like it."

Emily shook her head. "It doesn't. And that sign the little brown dog's got on says Fairtrade Fashion. But you can't have organic clothes, can you? That's stupid. Oh, we're moving…"

The bus pulled away, and even though the girls tried to peer back at the shop out of the rear window, they couldn't really see.

"I wonder if my mum went into Appleby today," Emily said excitedly. "She said she had shopping to do and she might have gone and had a look in there. I'll ask her."

Maya nodded. She was sure if she asked her mum or dad they'd take her to look – although people in the shop might recognise her mum. But she was still thinking about the Fairtrade thing. "If it *is* Fairtrade clothes…"

Emily beamed at her. "That would be a brilliant project. *Way* better than chocolate."

"Exactly! And hopefully nobody else will think of it." Maya looked sideways at Emily. "Ali and Lucy would be so jealous."

"Mmmm." Emily smiled happily. "Kicking themselves."

"Emily! Come on!" Toby was standing in front of them, pulling Emily's arm.

"Oh, I have to get off. See you tomorrow! Hey, do you realise we've just done our homework?" Emily called back as she hurried down the aisle.

Maya laughed, and waved goodbye to her as the bus set off again. She loved clothes, and spent a lot of her allowance on her favourite websites. Even if she didn't like dressing up to be photographed any more, she still enjoyed planning her outfits just as much as her mum did. The bad thing about Park Road School was its horrible uniform – a bright blue jumper that made Maya's red hair look gingery. Maya always changed as soon as she got home.

Luckily, because she was the only person who got dropped in her tiny village, the bus stopped outside her house and Mr Green would let her off if he could see someone waving from the front door. Maya hurried down the steps, wanting to go straight in and ask her mum if she'd spotted the new shop.

"I'll make you a snack," Anna called, as she turned to head back into the kitchen.

"Thanks, Anna." She gave her a hug, which she didn't always. "I'm going to see Mum, and then I've got to do some stuff on the computer for homework." She headed back into the hallway.

Almost all the signs of the photoshoot that morning had disappeared. The big living room at the back of the house was still frighteningly tidy when she peeped into it, and the extra pots of flowers that Mum had hired to brighten up the garden were still there, but that was it. Maya had a feeling the photographer had taken all the shots from the garden side anyway, so the pots had been useless.

"Mum!" she called.

"Upstairs," a muffled voice came back, and Maya raced up the stairs to find her.

"I'm just going to change," she told her mum, sticking her head round the door. "See you in a minute."

The yellow dress in the window of the new shop was still in Maya's mind, so she found herself grabbing a yellow T-shirt and a denim skirt. Then she hurried back to her mum's room.

"Mum, did you go into Appleby today at all?"

Her mum looked up from the computer. She was lying on her sofa reading emails on her laptop, and she looked tired, but she brightened up when she saw Maya.

"No, that interview went on for ages, and then I've had lots of work stuff to catch up on. Why?"

"There's a new shop." Maya perched on the edge of the sofa, leaning against her mum's shoulder. The stylist that morning had raved about their hair, how it was exactly the same colour, and she was right,

Maya noticed, seeing her own next to her mum's. She could hardly tell the difference. "A clothes shop, a really cool one. It's called Daisy. I spotted it when we were on the bus on the way home. There was a gorgeous dress…"

"Oh, I'll have to go and have a look." Her mum smiled. "Maybe buy you a present. They had girls' clothes, did they?"

"Yes, but have you ever heard of Fairtrade clothes, Mum? The window display said they sold Fairtrade, and it was all organic, too."

Her mum frowned. "That sounds a bit strange. More your kind of thing than mine." She shuddered a little. "It's probably all woven out of tree bark, or something."

Maya's mum wore much more designery stuff than Maya. She'd even modelled for a photoshoot years and years ago in a fur coat, which made Maya furious just thinking about it. Maya's mum teased her about looking like a hippy.

"It wasn't all tie-dye and long skirts, Mum. It looked great. But I can't work out the Fairtrade thing. If it really does mean Fairtrade clothes, it's the best timing. We have to do a project on it. The whole class is doing theirs on Fairtrade chocolate – we want to have something that's just us. This would be perfect!"

"It sounds much better than most school projects. No junk modelling?"

Maya gave her a Look. Maya's recycling bug had hit her in Year Two, when they'd had a teacher who was very concerned about the environment and did lots of work on green issues with the class. Maya had really got enthusiastic about it – so much that she had her only major fight with Macey, over Macey's junk model of a space station, which had been made out of plastic bottles, loo rolls and all sorts of odd bits. And a lot of silver paint.

Maya had gone a bit over the top with the class recycling competition, and several bits of space station had mysteriously vanished, including the astronauts' living quarters. Macey hadn't spoken to her for three weeks. They'd made up eventually, but Maya never stopped being into recycling – and solar power, and electric cars, and composting, and organic food. Her dad had said once that he felt like anything that was fun was bound to be "wasting the earth's resources" somehow. That was after Maya had argued with him for a solid hour about his new car.

"And we can do anything we like – Mr Finlay said to be imaginative. Maybe we could go and talk to

45

the people who run the shop about where they get the clothes from? Like a TV interview," Maya said thoughtfully. "We could even video it! But I don't know anything about Fairtrade fashion. I suppose I could just search for it online."

Her mum frowned. "Actually, I do remember reading something about it. Emma Watson, you know, the actress from *Harry Potter*, she's designed clothes for an ethical fashion company. We should look her up."

"Ethical fashion? Is that something else like Fairtrade?"

Her mum was nodding as she typed. "Mmm. No child labour."

"That happens with clothes too?" Maya asked anxiously. "Mr Finlay was showing us pictures of children harvesting cocoa beans today."

Maya's mum made a face. "Lots of clothes companies have been in trouble about it recently. There've been reports of children working in awful conditions, in India especially, and then the clothes they make being sold here really cheaply. Oh, here you are, look! This is the website."

"You're a star!" Maya hugged her, and started to read the webpage. "Wow. Jewellery as well. And look

46

at all those other links. Mum, can you send me this? I need to go and make some notes to show Emily and Poppy and Izzy tomorrow."

"Who's Izzy?" her mum asked.

"She's in our group for the project," Maya explained. "It was just going to be me and Emily and Poppy, but she didn't have anyone to work with…" Maya sighed. "I hope it's going to be OK. Emily was really annoyed with me for asking Izzy to be with us."

"Emily's sort of like that, though, isn't she? From what you've told me, anyway." Maya's mum looked a bit wistful, and Maya felt guilty. Her mum missed seeing Maya's friends too. She loved it when Macey came round for a sleepover. She never, ever moaned about it, but it was easy to see she wished Maya would have her new friends over sometimes.

"Mmm. Izzy's nice. She's very shy, I think. She doesn't get on that well with anyone in our class, and Ali's lot hate her." Maya laughed as her mum made a sort of disgusted growling noise. "What?"

"It's probably a good thing you won't let me pick you up from school, Maya. I'd quite happily strangle that Ali. She even looks like a little horror in your school photos. Something about those ponytails. And that smirk…"

"She's definitely the evillest person in our class. Izzy pretends it doesn't get to her, but she was really upset last time they were having a go at her." Maya stroked the ribbons sewn on to one of her mum's mad cushions. The sofa was covered in them. "I suppose we ought to have been nice to her before."

Her mum sighed. "Maybe. But you haven't had the easiest time, joining the school so late, and not knowing anyone. You do know how impressed Dad and I were, don't you? Most girls would have loved all the attention you got at Graham House."

Maya stared at her. "You didn't act impressed! You tried to make me stay!"

"I know we did. I wasn't sure if it was just a whim. You know, that you'd had another fight with Macey, and you were having a bit of a sulk. Then we realised you were really serious about it. Although I still think you'd be better off at Graham House, to be honest. All the computers, the music studio..."

"The horrible girls all gossiping and back-stabbing all the time," Maya put in.

"OK, OK." Her mum sighed. "Listen, Maya, thank you for this morning. Did you hate it?"

Maya wrinkled her nose. "I used to love the dressing up, and everyone fussing over me, but it's so fake, isn't it?"

Her mum shrugged.

"I'm not being nasty," Maya said quickly. "It just seems a bit pointless, that's all. Next week they'll be going on about somebody else's gorgeous house, and telling people they ought to have carpets like theirs instead."

"You didn't enjoy it even a little bit?" her mum asked, as though she found it hard to believe Maya hadn't. Maya could tell she was disappointed. Her mum would love it if Maya took after her as a singer, or an actress, but sometimes Maya felt like she didn't have a showbizzy bone in her body.

"Oh well," her mum murmured quietly. "It'll be very good for this new travel programme. Sorry, Maya. It's one of the downsides of the job." She hugged Maya close. "You looked lovely in the photos, though. That's the nice bit for me."

"I didn't look like me with all that make-up on," Maya muttered. "Which is good. I just hope no one from school recognises me. And if I ever do it again, Mum, no false eyelashes. They hurt." She fluttered her own short eyelashes and scowled, trying to cheer her mum up.

"I promise," her mum said solemnly, but she

49

was almost laughing again. "I couldn't believe how grown-up you sounded in the interview bit. She was impressed with you, the writer from the magazine. I suppose you're going to be a brilliant campaigner for something when you're older."

"Maybe." Maya was pretty sure that her mum would prefer a starry daughter, someone who danced as well as Emily, perhaps. Maya had seen her friend dance in the school play, and thought she was amazing. Still. Her mum was good at not forcing her into that kind of thing. She could cope with the odd photoshoot here and there.

She sighed, and leaned back against her mum's shoulder. "I wish you weren't going off working tomorrow. It's so nice being able to talk to you about school stuff."

"Well, I'm only in Italy for two weeks, then I'll be back for a bit. And Dad's not coming. He loves hearing about all your friends."

Maya sniffed. "Yes, but I can't see Dad being much use on a fashion project."

Her mum tried to keep a straight face. "He might be..." but then she gave up, and sniggered. "No, all right, maybe not. I threw away his tracksuit bottoms last night, you know. I actually buried them in the bottom of the wheelie bin. Otherwise I'm certain he would have answered the door to the magazine people in them this morning."

Maya laughed. "What did he say?"

Her mum looked shifty. "I haven't actually told him... He spent a while looking for them this morning. Don't you dare tell him, Maya! He's got so many pairs of perfectly good trousers. He didn't need to be living in a pair with holes in."

"And paint stains," Maya added.

"*And* they didn't fit him properly in the first place," her mum agreed. "Oh, I'm going to miss you, Maya. I don't suppose the school would let you come too, even if we said it was educational."

Maya closed her eyes for a moment. She'd been to Italy before with Mum and Dad, for holidays. She loved it there. It was always sunny, and full of delicious smells. And the food was fab, even for vegetarians. They could not tell school... She could say she had chicken pox. "It would be nice," she whispered. Then she shook her head. "But I've got this project. I think it's going to be really good." She looked up apologetically at her mum. "I'll miss you too, though."

"I know you can't come really," her mum said with

a sigh. "I suppose I ought to pack, we're flying out tomorrow."

Maya frowned. "Oh, Mum. Couldn't you get the Eurostar?"

Her mum looked away, and Maya sat up. "Tell me it's not a private jet!"

"I didn't book it, Maya! The production company's organised it because there aren't a lot of scheduled flights, it's such a small airport. And I will mention the tree thing a lot. I promise I will personally say it to every single camera."

"You can't just call it the tree thing," Maya grumped. "Carbon offsetting, Mum. It isn't just planting trees."

Whenever Maya's mum flew, she donated money through a website which used it to pay for green projects. Maya did it, too, whenever they went on holiday. Which was quite a lot. She was pretty sure she'd paid for several trees out of her allowance. The carbon offsetting website she'd found used the money to put solar panels on houses in Africa too, to stop more fossil fuels being burned.

"Don't forget to do it, will you?" she asked her mum, getting up.

"I'm doing it now! Look. Carbon Future, I'm on

the website. I'm typing the flights in now." Her mum tapped the keys triumphantly. "See?"

"OK." Maya nodded. "Thanks, Mum! I'm going to work on the project now."

"Wow, that must be at least six trees' worth," her mum muttered. "Couldn't we just plant them at the bottom of the garden, Maya? I could have a little forest. We could have fairy lights in them for parties. Solar-powered ones," she added quickly.

"Sorry, Mum, I don't think it works like that…"

FOUR

Maya opened the chat message from her mum, and clicked on the link to the fashion blog she'd sent. Along with about fifty kisses. Maya grinned, and held down the x key to send even more back, before she settled down to read the blog.

It was mostly about Emma Watson, and the clothing collection she'd designed, but it explained a little bit about the company she'd worked with. It definitely said they were a Fairtrade fashion producer. Maya bounced a little with excitement. So they could do their project on fashion! She couldn't wait to talk to the others about it tomorrow. Maybe she could ring Emily now? No, she'd find out a little bit more first. She read through to the end of the article, and then followed a link to the clothes website. For once, she didn't really want to look at the clothes themselves, although she noticed some very cool earrings. She was more interested in how they were made. And who was making them, especially.

Maya guessed that the Fairtrade clothes meant that the workers got paid more, but she wasn't sure if there was anything else they needed to know to decide about their project. The photos Mr Finlay had shown them that afternoon at school of the children harvesting cocoa had made her really sad, but Maya wasn't sure how children would be able to make clothes – after all, clothes were made in factories. How could children work sewing machines and things like that? Her grandma had a sewing machine, and she'd shown Maya how it worked. It was *really* complicated.

Then again, that little boy harvesting the cocoa had been using a knife that looked dangerous even for an adult. And her mum had said that children had been working in factories in India.

She went back to the search box and typed in "child labour clothes".

A whole long list of matches came up, pages and pages of them. Mostly they were newspaper articles, talking about the companies who'd been discovered using child labour. Maya's eyes widened. She knew the names of almost all those shops! She loved to

go clothes shopping with her mum, although they couldn't go shopping anywhere around Millford now that Maya didn't want to be recognised as India Kell's daughter. Even if her mum wore huge sunglasses, she almost always got spotted, and then Maya usually ducked behind a clothes rail and pretended she wasn't with her. But it was their favourite way to spend a day together, pottering around the shops – not always buying that much, just trying on and talking, and stopping for Maya's mum to have coffee, and Maya to have a milkshake.

Maya read through one of the articles, from a few years ago. This was what her mum had been talking about. It sounded as though there'd been a television programme, with secret footage of what were called sweatshops – which were factories where the workers were treated really badly and made to work long hours. Even all night sometimes. And some of these workers were only nine or ten. Younger than her. Maya swallowed. Why would they want to use children? She didn't understand.

She read further on, and sniffed. She felt like she was going to start crying over her computer in the middle of her bedroom, which was just stupid. It was all about money! Children didn't need to be paid as much as adults – that was why so many of them were employed in the factories, just to save even more money. It was so unfair.

Maya sat up straight suddenly with a gasp, and grabbed the back of her yellow T-shirt, wriggling it round so she could see the label. She'd thought so – she and her mum had bought it in one of the shops mentioned in the article. It could have been a child her own age sewing all the little beads and sequins on to the flower pattern on the front.

Hurriedly, she pulled it off, and changed it for another one from the drawer – she didn't know for certain where this pink one had been made either, though.

She spread the yellow T-shirt out on her bed, and stared at it, looking at the pretty design on the front. It was so delicate – embroidery, and hundreds of glittering sequins and beads. She remembered buying it. It hadn't been very expensive, and she'd been surprised, because it looked so special. She'd used some money her gran had given her for her birthday. She wouldn't ever know exactly who'd made it. But the website she'd just been reading said the shop this T-shirt came from had actually admitted they'd used child workers. Children had been working in the

57

factories they used in Delhi, which was in India. They claimed they hadn't known about it, and they weren't using those factories any more. They'd stopped using them as soon as they found out.

Maya frowned. So what happened to all those children? There was a photo with the article, of a little girl sitting cross-legged sewing beads on to a vest top. She looked so tired, and there was a pile of more vests next to her – Maya couldn't tell if they were ones she'd already done, or what she still had to sew. The caption explained that she had been working at the factory for two years, because her parents couldn't afford to send her to school, and she needed to earn money to help her family. Maya wished she knew what the girl's name was, and what had happened to her after the clothes shop stopped using her factory. It sounded like such good news – but if her family had really needed the money the girl was earning, then it must have been terrible for them if she suddenly didn't have a job any more.

She's probably working in the same place, and being paid even less, because now the factory doesn't have an expensive shop as a customer any more, Maya thought miserably. *She would have to work even longer hours. Or maybe she lost her job, and her whole family went hungry.*

Maya looked at the T-shirt unhappily, knowing that she'd probably never want to wear it again – but that felt almost worse. Someone had worked so hard for it, and she'd never even known.

She clicked on a link to another page. More children! She was sure they were younger than her, too. Maya hated even looking at the photos – she couldn't imagine how frightening it must be to know that your family needed you to work, just so they had enough to eat. She sat staring at the computer, sniffing, and trying not to cry.

The door swung open a little, and Maya jumped, glancing up from the laptop. Her eyes were blurry, so Henry looked even furrier than usual as he trotted over to her bed, and leaped up. "Hey," Maya muttered, fussing over him, rubbing him behind the ears and under the chin, so that he purred blissfully and sat down on the keyboard of her laptop, jealous that she was paying it so much attention.

Maya gulped and laughed at the same time as the computer beeped warningly, and Henry glared at it. She scooped him closer to her, and closed the laptop lid. She didn't want to read any more right now anyway. It was too sad. At least she could turn it off.

"I'm not sure this project is going to be as fun as we

thought it was," she muttered to Henry, but he only purred, and banged his nose into her cheek the way he did when he wanted more petting.

Henry was a black and white Norwegian Forest cat, and he officially belonged to Maya's mum. But Henry had decided he was Maya's now, whether she liked it or not. He was very big – not fat, but heavy, and muscly for a cat. He had long black fur, and a tail like a feather duster. He was not a vegetarian. Maya had once ordered some vegetarian cat food online for him, but he had stared at his bowl in horror, and then gone out and caught a mouse. He left most of the mouse on the kitchen floor, and Anna had trodden in it in her new slippers. Maya decided to stop experimenting after that.

"What if it's just too sad?" she asked Henry, frowning. That was stupid. She already knew about the sweatshops now. Pretending that she didn't care wasn't going to work. She had to do something instead.

"Did you find out anything useful?" Her mum was standing in the doorway. "Oh, Maya, what's wrong?"

"It's so awful. Those factories." Maya sniffed.

Her mum sighed. "I'm sorry, Maya. I should have looked at it with you. Maybe this isn't a good idea for a project," her mum said doubtfully. "Perhaps you should do chocolate, like the rest of your class."

But even though Maya had been thinking the same a few minutes before, she shook her head firmly. "No. We have to tell people about it." Then she sighed. "But the only people we'll be telling are the others in our class. That isn't much use. We need to make our project really important somehow, so that people notice it."

"Could you do a school assembly? I'd be surprised if your teacher hadn't thought about something like that already," her mum suggested.

Maya nodded, but she'd been thinking bigger than that somehow.

"Anyway, when I'm back from this trip, Maya, maybe I can help with the project. I'm useless at numeracy and the other stuff you bring home from school but at least I know a bit about clothes!" Her mum gave her a hug. "I'm really pleased that you worry about things like this, but don't spend the whole time getting upset about it, will you?"

Maya shook her head. What was the point in crying? She needed to do something, not just be sad. "Thanks for saying you'll help."

"As long as you don't want me to draw anything,"

her mum warned. "You know how bad I am at it. Anyway, what I was coming to say was that I've told Neil to clean out the pool, and refill it – it's getting summery enough to use it now."

Maya's eyes brightened, and she felt a little jolt of excitement, just for a second. The pool! It was one of her favourite things. It was wonderful for sitting by on a hot day, but since it was heated, she loved swimming in it even when it was a bit chilly. She just stayed under the warm water, with only her nose and eyes out in the air. Then she remembered.

Her mum noticed her face and sighed. "It isn't really that bad," she said, sounding slightly annoyed.

"Yes, it is," Maya muttered. "It's a disaster. All the energy we waste heating it! And the chlorine!" *But it's so much fun*, a little voice inside her was saying. *And I try so hard all the time, making everybody recycle, and moaning at Dad about driving the car. Isn't it worse if the pool's there and no one even swims in it?*

"You know you love swimming, Maya. Don't be so dismal. You could invite your friends round to swim, while your dad and I are away." Her mum smiled rather sadly. "I wouldn't be here for them to recognise."

Maya gave her a little hug.

"The pool's there anyway, Maya. Just make sure you get Anna or Neil to be around if you use it."

Maya nodded. She knew she shouldn't, but it was so lovely and warm, lying there looking up at the sky, and the clouds streaming past. Maya loved the way swimming made her feel – all light and floaty and happy. She supposed she could always save up for another few trees...

Emily raced up the aisle of the bus to her, trailing all her bags, and Toby and James's too. She dropped them on a seat in front of Maya, and sighed, rolling her eyes. "We had to go back for James's coat. I swear, we need a checklist and they're not allowed out of the front door without everything on it. How can you lose a coat between the hall and the front gate?"

"You made it, though," Maya said comfortingly, picking up Emily's coat as it threatened to slide down the aisle.

Emily sighed. "Neither of them's got a water bottle, and I don't know where they are. On somebody's garden wall, I should think. We found Toby's outside the hairdresser last week. And we hadn't even *been* to the hairdresser!"

Maya giggled. She could see Toby and James

further down the bus. It looked as though they were having a competition for who could bounce the highest. Emily looked too, and then huddled down in her seat. "I'm not related to them, really," she muttered.

"Did you talk to your mum about the new shop?" Maya asked hopefully. "Had she been in there?"

Emily brightened up. "Yes! And she said it was gorgeous, and not as expensive as she'd expected it would be. She bought me some really nice hairbands, but I'm not wearing them for school in case I lose them."

"Did she say anything about it being Fairtrade stuff?"

Emily nodded. "That was why she went in. They had Fairtrade baby clothes in the window too – I don't think we had time to spot those. She bought some cute leggings for Sukie, and a little T-shirt that says *Save My Planet* on it. And money from them goes to a project in Bangladesh. Toby and James got really grumpy because she didn't buy anything for them, but Mum said she'd be quite happy to go back and buy them hairbands or pink leggings too, and they shut up." She smiled to herself, and then sighed. "But I didn't get a chance to look anything up on the computer. I'd just about finished my maths homework from yesterday, and then it was tea, and then we had to take Toby to Beavers, and then Mum said would I look after Sukie while she managed to have a bath, and then when Dad got home he wanted to do some work on it." Emily gasped for breath. "He said I could have it tonight, though. And I did check our cupboards. Fairtrade rice, and sugar, but that was all."

Maya shook her head. "You know, yesterday at lunch I was wishing I had brothers and sisters too, but I don't think I could cope with your lot. You don't get a minute." *And I don't have to share my gorgeous purple laptop with anyone*, she added to herself. She didn't want to gloat over that to Emily. But she felt a bit ashamed of herself for moaning about being an only child.

"I'm never lonely, that's for sure." Emily shrugged, and grinned at her. "So did you find anything?"

"Yes…" Maya sighed. "You know how the stuff Mr Finlay showed us about the cocoa harvest was really sad?"

Emily nodded, frowning. "This was too?"

"Worse, almost. It was scary, Ems." Maya stared down at her fingers. "Kids our age, stuck in these

horrible factories." Maya felt her cheeks burning. "And there was a list of clothes shops that have been caught out using child labour. I was wearing a T-shirt from one of them while I was looking stuff up on the computer. I felt so guilty."

Emily put an arm round her. "But you didn't know that!"

Maya shrugged. "It feels like I should have done. I remember being really pleased about how cheap the T-shirt was, because it was so pretty. And even if it wasn't made by someone our age, it was probably made in a sweatshop, where the workers weren't paid enough."

"Wonder where our school uniform was made…" Emily muttered. "Mum usually gets it in the big supermarket just outside Millford. She says there's no point buying expensive stuff for school, it just gets trashed."

"I didn't even think about school uniform." Maya's eyes widened. "But it's getting cheaper and cheaper, isn't it? There was a TV ad for uniform that only cost four pounds, back at the beginning of the year. Four pounds! That's nothing. It's like – a sandwich and a drink in a café!" She frowned. "How can you get someone to make a shirt and a skirt and a jumper, and then ship it to this country, and then sell it for that much? It just doesn't *work*."

"Our jumpers come from school, though," Emily reminded her. "We have to order them from the office. They wouldn't use manky factories, would they?"

Maya shrugged. "Do you think Mrs Brooker in the office knows about Fairtrade cotton and sweatshops? She's usually more worried about tracking down people who haven't paid their dinner money."

"You're probably right." Emily suddenly looked worried. "Oh, no, it's OK, we've definitely paid this week's; I remember handing it in." She sighed with relief. "And I bet it isn't up to the school where the clothes come from, they just choose from a catalogue, or something. If they didn't know to worry about Fairtrade, they wouldn't even think about it, would they?"

"Nope. We could ask, though. Don't you think that could be part of our project somehow? We could try and get school to use Fairtrade jumpers. Send a petition to Mrs Angel!" Maya's eyes were sparkling. Finally, it felt like there was something they could do, even if it was only little.

"Mr Finlay did say to be creative. Think big…"

Emily said doubtfully. "I'm not sure he meant go and harass Mrs Brooker, though." She shrugged. "I'm up for it. It might be nice to be the one in Mrs Angel's office for once. I bet she's really sick of Toby and James."

The girls hurried off the bus, and Maya saw Poppy over by the door to their classroom. She was trying to plait a daisy chain into her hair.

"We've got the most brilliant idea for our project!" Emily told her proudly.

"Oh good!" Poppy dropped the daisy chain, and looked over her shoulder. "Izzy's over there," she murmured. "I nearly went and sat with her, but she's reading a book, and she looks really grumpy, so I didn't want to interrupt her."

Emily snorted, grabbed Poppy's hand and towed her across to Izzy. "Me and Maya have got a really good idea for the project," she snapped, dumping her bag at Izzy's feet. Maya gave a tiny sigh. Emily clearly still wasn't happy about the extra member of their group. But hey, at least she wasn't trying to leave Izzy out.

Izzy practically dropped her book, and Maya felt really sorry for her. It was probably the first time anyone had come and talked to her before school in ages.

"The school bus went home past a new clothes shop," she explained. "Selling Fairtrade clothes!" She'd lowered her voice to a whisper, and she glanced round to check the other girls weren't hanging around. She really didn't want anyone nicking their idea again.

Izzy was frowning. "How can you have Fairtrade clothes? Fairtrade's for food."

"That's what we said!" Emily burst out, looking slightly annoyed at having to agree with Izzy. "Fairtrade and organic – it doesn't sound like clothes, does it? But Maya looked it up, and you can. It's to do with who's making them, a bit like the chocolate. And loads of children make clothes too."

"There were really sad photos," Maya told them. "Then Emily had a brainwave on the bus – we don't know whether our school jumpers were made in sweatshops – that's what the really awful factories are called. So we could try and find out, as part of our project! And if they're not Fairtade, we're going to campaign that they ought to be."

She looked anxiously at Poppy and Izzy.

"What do you think? We didn't mean to take it all over – it was just that we happened to see the shop."

But Poppy was looking really excited. "That's such a good idea! Do you think we could change the colour of our uniform at the same time?" she added hopefully. "I hate this blue. Green would be much better. Or purple!" She sighed apologetically as they all glared at her. "All right! I suppose that isn't really the point…"

Maya looked at Izzy. She hadn't said anything, and they hardly knew her. Maya really hoped she liked the idea. "What do you think?"

Izzy nodded. "It sounds good. I looked up Fairtrade last night, all the different things you can get, and I remember now it did say cotton, but I didn't really take much notice of it. I was still thinking about doing something to do with food." She glanced up at Maya hopefully. "I can find out about the organic bit, if we want to put that in too. My dad might know something, he's really into growing organic stuff in the garden. He'd help me do some research, even if he doesn't know to start with."

Maya could have hugged her. She almost did, except that Izzy looked so prickly sometimes, Maya thought she might not like it.

"This is going to be so good!" she said, and compromised by giving Izzy the most enormous smile.

FIVE

"I really want to see this shop," Poppy said. "I bet if I told my mum that we had to go and see it for a project, she'd take me. She might even take all of us, if I asked really nicely. And I've got some birthday money I could spend."

"Do you think your mum and dad would let you come too, Izzy?" Maya asked.

"I just live with my dad," Izzy muttered. Maya stared at her feet, feeling embarrassed. She hadn't known that. But when none of the girls asked Izzy why, or where her mum was, even though they all wanted to, she gave them a nervous smile. "He won't mind. And he owes me weeks of allowance. Maybe I could buy something too." She looked as though she was expecting to be told that she certainly couldn't, Maya thought. She really had been properly squashed by Ali's lot.

"A shopping trip!" Emily beamed. "And not with Toby and James hiding under the clothes rails, so Mum goes into a panic. I'm definitely coming. Although we're not really going just to shop, of course," she added, her voice suddenly serious. But she was trying not to laugh.

"Of course not," everyone chorused, trying to sound as though they weren't excited at all.

Maya got her phone out, without thinking, and Izzy's eyes widened. "You've got your own mobile?"

Maya looked up from the screen. "Oh. Um, yes. It was a present. My parents are away a lot – they send me texts. I was just going to put your number in it, so that I could call you, let you know when we're going to meet up to go to the shop."

Izzy nodded, but she was still looking at Maya curiously. "Why didn't you say you had a phone when Ali was going on and on about hers last week? Yours looks a lot nicer."

Maya shrugged. She could hardly say that she didn't want to draw attention to herself.

Poppy giggled, and scrabbled in her bag for a notebook. "The rest of us just use a bit of paper. Give us your number, Izzy. I'll get my mum to call your dad, if she says yes to taking us."

Izzy nodded, pink-cheeked. "I'd really like to go," she said quietly, as she wrote her phone number down. Maya had a feeling that, for Izzy, it was a big commitment to make. If she was brave enough to say that sort of thing, someone could turn round and laugh at her, and tell her she wasn't wanted.

"They had such nice stuff in the window," she told Izzy encouragingly. "I tried to have another good look this morning. There was a blue T-shirt, wasn't there, Emily? I think you'd look good in pale blue." Maya eyed the sleeve of her school jumper and sighed. "Poppy is right. This doesn't really do much for anyone."

Izzy didn't say anything, and when Maya glanced back at her, Izzy was looking like a rabbit caught in some headlights. It was as though she was expecting Maya to turn her perfectly normal comments into some sort of bitchy, backstabbing nastiness any second.

"You see! It would be a brilliant chance to get a better uniform!" Poppy folded her arms triumphantly. "If we want to change the jumpers anyway. But I can't see Mrs Angel going for it. She's always saying how smart we look."

Mr Finlay gave them all some time after break to talk about what they'd found out, and Maya tried to describe the stuff she'd been looking up.

"You're all very quiet." Mr Finlay perched on the edge of their table, looking at them all staring at Maya's page of notes. "Did you not find much? I liked your idea of doing something different."

Emily shook her head. "It isn't that. Maya's got loads of stuff for the project. We just don't know what to do with it yet. And it's kind of miserable."

"We have got your brilliant idea," Poppy reminded her. "But that's a bit secret," she told Mr Finlay apologetically. "We need to work out how we're going to do it first."

"Well, as long as you're working on something, that's fine."

"Would you be able to make an appointment for us to go and see Mrs Angel? Maybe at the beginning of next week?" Maya asked him hopefully, and Mr Finlay stared at her. "I suppose so… As part of your project?" he asked, rather doubtfully.

The girls all nodded at him, and Mr Finlay looked slightly worried, as though he wasn't sure what he'd let himself in for.

♡

Poppy's mum was keen on the idea of a shopping trip too, and she said she didn't mind picking all the girls up. Maya was waiting outside her house for ages before they arrived – she'd been up really early, picking out what she wanted to wear, and trying not to put on anything that came from one of the shops she'd read about.

"Guess what I found out!" Emily told her proudly, as soon as Maya got in, squashing up between Emily and Izzy in the back seat with a tiny sigh. They'd been sitting as far apart from each other as they possibly could.

Maya shook her head, trying to wriggle enough room to do her seat belt up. "What?"

"There's a whole campaign about Fairtrade school uniform! I looked it up, when Dad finally let me have the computer. It's called Wear Fair. I printed this off. It's a petition we can get everyone in school to sign, to say we want Fairtrade uniform!"

"Wow…" Maya looked at the sheet. "To the chair of the school governors… Do we have those?"

Izzy nodded. "My dad's one. I'll make him say yes!"

"And there's lots of other stuff on the website too. If Mr Finlay would let us have an assembly, there's a video we could play. Lots of things."

"A whole assembly of just us?" Poppy asked doubtfully.

"I bet we could," Emily shrugged. "Why not?"

"They'd probably say we had to do just a bit of it, so all the groups can say something," Maya pointed out. "But at least we'd have time to ask everyone to sign this."

"I think we're nearly there, aren't we?" Poppy's mum asked, glancing at the map print-out that Poppy was holding up for her in the front seat.

Maya looked up from the petition. "Oh yes. It's the next left. The main road through Appleby." She peered excitedly out of the window as Poppy's mum drove along slowly. "There it is!"

The shop looked just as good close up as it had from the school-bus window, and the girls hurried to get out of the car without squashing each other.

"Such nice things," Poppy sighed, practically pressing her nose up against the window. "And organic essential oils too!" she said to her mum, who was quite interested in alternative therapies, though not as wholeheartedly as Poppy was.

"We could just go in..." her mum pointed out, laughing at them. "You don't have to act like you're

starving to death in front of a cake shop."

Maya shivered. Her mum had a saying about a goose walking over her grave, and she could feel the funny little feet right now. Poppy's mum hadn't meant anything, but she'd reminded Maya about all those children harvesting cocoa, who probably never ate a chocolate bar. *We're trying to help*, she told herself firmly, following the others in.

She almost forgot the strange feeling when she finally got inside the shop. It was so beautiful. The walls had little daisies on them here and there, and the cute stuffed dogs from the window were scattered around too. One of them had a basket in his mouth, holding the hairbands Emily had told her about.

A friendly-looking dark-haired woman was reading a book behind the till, but she smiled delightedly at them as they piled in.

"Hello! The girls' section is mostly in the next room. Just let me know if you need any help, won't you?"

The back room had even more flowers, and a sky painted with little clouds and butterflies. And the clothes were amazing, even better than they'd looked in the window. "I wish I hadn't bought all those DVDs in the Easter holidays," Emily said. "I think I can only have one thing. But look at this skirt! And these jeans are even nicer, almost…" She was ferreting through the racks eagerly, and sighing with longing.

"But the thing is, Ems, if you're only having one thing, is it better to only try on one thing so you don't fall in love with lots of things, or should you try on everything in the shop to make sure you get the absolute best thing there is?" Poppy wondered, holding up an embroidered gypsy skirt, and flouncing out the ruffles.

"You lost me after the second 'thing'," Emily told her. "But I think I know what you mean. Definitely try all of it."

"I think so too." Maya nodded, which was quite difficult given the size of the pile of clothing she was holding.

"Look on the bright side," Izzy said, raising one eyebrow, "at least you don't have to try on the hairbands, since your mum already got you some. But don't forget there were bags in the other room. And jewellery."

Emily sighed. "You are so not helping!" But at least she didn't glare at Izzy this time. "Aren't you going to try anything on?" she asked, staring at her in surprise.

Izzy shrugged a little. "I don't know…" She looked a bit embarrassed.

"You'd look really nice in this." Maya passed Izzy the pale blue T-shirt she'd told her about before. "Really. It's the same sort of colour as your eyes."

Izzy looked even more embarrassed now, but a smidge pleased as well. "You think so?" she muttered shyly. "I wasn't going to buy anything – I did bring some money, but I thought I'd just look at the labels, see what they said about where they were made."

"But we're going to do that as well!" Maya told her, laughing. "It doesn't mean we can't all have fun trying the clothes on first. I even brought my mum's little recorder thing, so we could ask the lady out the front if she wouldn't mind being interviewed."

Izzy sighed. "I'm just not very good at shopping."

"I'm sure this lot could give you lessons." Poppy's mum snorted with laughter. "But don't boss Izzy into something she doesn't want, girls."

"Oh, we won't!" Maya promised. But she was frowning. How could Izzy not like shopping? She was wearing jeans and a T-shirt – actually, they all were, only Maya's jeans were green, and Poppy's were super-short frayed cut-offs, with stripy leggings underneath. Izzy's were pretty plain, but she didn't

80

look like somebody who didn't care what she wore.

"Mostly I get my clothes out of catalogues," Izzy explained. "Dad doesn't really like going to clothes shops. He tries! But I can tell he's feeling embarrassed. And it's fun getting the parcels…" But she was looking at the rails of clothes wistfully.

"Catalogues are great," Maya agreed. "But it's nice to try things on too. Hey, we should take turns! Like a fashion show! Everyone put on an outfit, and then we'll all help each other choose." She sighed at her pile. "I definitely need help. Actually, Izzy, this skirt would look good with that blue T-shirt too." She edged it off the top of the pile. "That's better. Now I can actually carry it all."

Poppy glanced around. "The changing rooms are over here, look. Two of them. You'd better go first, Emily, you've got loads."

"I know, I just liked it all." Emily sighed. "Anyway, that's a huge pile you've got, you'd better start trying on as well."

Emily's first outfit, a little flowery dress, was a definite no. "I'm not sure about this," she told the others, as she came out of the cubicle. "It's too cutesy."

"It doesn't look like you," Maya agreed. "Try the denim skirt on instead."

"Your go first, remember?" Emily pointed out.

Maya nodded. "Or you, Izzy. Do you want to try those on?"

"Izzy can have this cubicle," Poppy said, pulling back the curtain and stepping out. "What do you think?"

"Oooh!" Maya sighed admiringly. "So nice!" It was the gypsy skirt Poppy had been admiring, in flounces of spots and stripes, and it looked fab.

"Yeah, I like it too." Poppy twirled, giggling as the skirt whirled round. "Really like it… Go on, Izzy, try your things on, I need to think. This is going to take almost all my birthday money."

Izzy went hesitantly into the cubicle, and Maya and Poppy exchanged a worried glance. Maya hoped they weren't forcing her into dressing up. She looked round for Poppy's mum, wondering if they should ask her advice, but she'd gone into the other room to look at the bags.

But when Izzy sidled out a couple of minutes later, she looked half-pleased, half-frightened.

"Why are you looking like that?" Emily demanded, not bothering to be tactful, as usual.

Poppy stepped in quickly. "It's great. It really suits you!"

Izzy stared at her, as though she was waiting for something else.

"It does look nice, Izzy," Maya promised. "Don't you believe us?"

Poppy frowned. "Did someone say mean stuff to you in a shop, or something? You look like you think we're going to be rude about you."

Izzy glared at the floor, hugging her arms around the pretty blue T-shirt. "Ali. The last time Dad really made an effort to take me shopping was for my birthday. It was just bad luck that she happened to be in the same shop. She was so horrible…" Izzy's voice filled with tears, and she gulped. "I can't cry on the clothes!"

Maya hugged her. She didn't care if Izzy didn't look like a hugging person. "It doesn't matter, because you should buy that T-shirt anyway. It looks so good. I mean it. And Ali has a nose like an ugly dog, Izzy, just remember that when she's being mean."

Izzy spluttered, halfway between tears and giggling.

"You see! She does! You know it too!" Maya told her triumphantly. She elbowed Emily and gave her a glare. Couldn't she see that this was more important

than her squabble with Izzy?

"She really does," Emily said solemnly. "And she always smells like an accident in a body-spray factory."

Izzy snorted, her hand over her mouth. "Stop it!" she wheezed. "I'll be sick."

"OK. But promise you'll get the T-shirt. Unless there's something nicer," Maya told her firmly.

Izzy nodded. "You try your stuff on."

Maya tried on her favourite thing first – a long T-shirt, with a belt to go round it that was covered in little embroidered birds and flowers. The label said it was organic cotton, and it had been made in India.

"That's pretty!" Izzy told her, as she came out. She was still sniffing a little, but she looked much happier, and she was sharing a chair with Poppy while they looked through a basket of bead necklaces. It was the friendliest Maya had ever seen her look.

"It's good with the belt," Emily agreed.

By the time they'd all tried on everything, Maya's pile had gone down to the T-shirt and belt, and a cool printed scarf. Izzy was getting the T-shirt and skirt, and Poppy had stuck to the gypsy skirt. Emily was still trying to decide.

"Do you want to try some bits on again?" Maya

asked. "I really like this fashion show thing. We should all go shopping together always!"

Emily sighed. "I don't think it will help. I like all these. Maybe we can talk to the owner of the shop about Fairtrade clothes before we buy things, and then I'll decide."

But Maya hardly heard her. She was staring at the clothes rails with an amazed expression on her face, which slowly turned into a delighted smile.

"I think I've just had a stunningly brilliant idea!"

"What? Is it a way for me to decide what to get? I'm not just tossing a coin, Maya." Emily folded her arms firmly.

"No, no, no! I think we should have a fashion show!" Maya sat down on one of the madly painted wooden chairs with a thump, frowning at her feet. "Just like we did now… Maybe not just the girls' clothes, though, we could get people to wear the adults' stuff. We could charge people to come in – just a little. We could send the money to one of the Fairtrade projects. And if everyone from school came, and their parents, they'd all see the gorgeous Fairtrade clothes, and they'd know about them then, wouldn't they? People would buy them if they knew more about them, or at least sometimes they would."

Izzy nodded. "We hadn't even heard of Fairtrade clothes – at least people would know there was something they could do."

Emily frowned. "But how could we have a fashion show? Do you mean we have to make clothes? We can't."

Maya shook her head. "No. Let's ask the lady out there. We could borrow these clothes. We'd look after them."

Poppy twirled her hair around her finger. "Do you think she'd let us?"

"We can only ask." Maya shrugged. "The worst she can do is say no."

"How are you girls doing?" The lady from the shop was leaning on the archway between the two rooms. "Your mum's decided to buy a handbag," she told Poppy.

Poppy grinned. "She loves bags. She'll have to hide it from my dad. Last time she came home with another one, he made her say if she bought any more she had to clear out one of the ones she'd already got."

"I heard that! Don't you dare tell him, Poppy Jane Martin!" Poppy's mum called from the other room.

"Bags too…" Emily sighed at the pile of things she was holding.

The shop owner nodded. "It's a women's cooperative in the Philippines, they make the bags out of juice cartons. You know, those foil pouch ones that are completely non-biodegradable, and just end up in landfill. The company actually started as an environmental project." She smiled, spotting Poppy's doubtful face. Maya guessed Poppy was a bit worried about what her mum was buying. "They do clean the pouches very carefully before they stitch them into bags. They don't look like rubbish."

"Oh!" Izzy smiled. "I saw them on the way in, the cute bags with the fruit on? I didn't realise they were drinks cartons."

"Exactly. Look, they're through here." She led the girls through to look at the display in the main shop, where Poppy's mum was holding two bags and dithering.

"Aren't they lovely?"

"They make gorgeous jewellery too, I'm just waiting for a delivery of that. It's made out of recycled magazines."

"That sounds amazing." Maya stroked one of the bags admiringly. "Oh, look, lunchboxes!" Anna had

been complaining that Maya's lunchbox was falling apart, but Maya really liked it. But she would love a new one like this. "Sorry, I'm putting the T-shirt back." She had enough money for a lunchbox as well, but she knew she got a lot more allowance than the others, and she didn't want to make it too obvious.

"They are great," Emily agreed.

Maya beamed at the shop owner hopefully as she picked up her lunchbox. "I don't suppose you've ever considered having a fashion show?" she asked. "Tara," she added, noticing that the lady had a pretty embroidered name-badge pinned on her dress.

Tara smiled. "Are you all volunteering to model?"

She didn't sound as though she was taking them very seriously, and Maya tried not to sigh. "No, thank you. We're interested in Fairtrade clothes. We're trying to get our school to switch to a Fairtrade uniform as well. We were wondering if we could organise a fashion show, to – er –" Maya tried to remember the phrases she'd seen on the websites she'd looked at. "To raise awareness," she added quickly. "Not just the children's clothes, the ladies' stuff too."

"My mum could model her bag," Poppy suggested, with a giggle, and her mum pretended to bat her with it.

Tara was looking more interested now. "I've actually been thinking about something like that."

"We could ask if our school would let us use the hall," Izzy put in. "We could send letters home to all the parents about it."

Tara was smiling. "I'd really like to try and raise some extra money for one of the groups we buy from. What gave you girls the idea of doing all this?" She sounded a little surprised, Maya thought. As though she wasn't used to people their age wanting to organise things.

"We're studying Fairtrade." Maya saw Emily blink at her, but she didn't want to say it was a school project. Studying sounded more serious somehow. "We've been doing some research. And then we saw your shop. It was luck, really," she admitted. "We actually want to *do* something, not just write about Fairtrade stuff."

"Could you let us borrow clothes from the shop for a show?" Izzy asked. "If we sold tickets, you could give the money to the group you were talking about."

"That would be amazing," Tara agreed. "They're trying to raise money to build a school. They're the ones who make these T-shirts." She stroked the blue T-shirt Izzy was carrying. "All this printing is done

by hand, you see. It's a group in Bangladesh – they want their workers to be able to survive in their own villages, instead of having to move to the cities, which are really overcrowded."

"We should put lots of their clothes in the show then," Maya suggested. "I don't know if our school would let you sell clothes there. But we could ask. And even if they don't, you could put a leaflet on all the chairs."

"If your school will let us use the hall, I'd love to do it." Tara looked shell-shocked, but really pleased.

Maya and the others looked at each other happily. It was actually going to happen!

"Now we just have to get Mrs Angel to agree…" Emily pointed out.

SIX

"If we're going to talk to Mrs Angel, we need to look really organised," Izzy explained. "And we need to be able to answer any questions she's got. So I looked this stuff up on the net. It's sort of a how-to-put-together-an-event info sheet."

"Wow... Show producer... Backstage manager... We haven't got enough people for all of this," Poppy said worriedly, leaning over their table to stare at the list Izzy had printed out.

"I think a lot of the jobs can be put together," Izzy explained. "And Tara will do some of it, won't she? We don't have to do all this bit about finding outfits. And she mentioned getting her daughter to find models at the sixth-form college. But we have to decide when we do the show – not the date, that'll be up to Mrs Angel, I suppose, but what time. If we want parents to come, it's got to be after school, or in the evening."

"Evening, definitely," Poppy said. "My mum couldn't come if it was after school, not unless she got an afternoon off work." Poppy went to after-school club most days.

"Yes, but if we have it in the evening, we might need more than just the fashion show," Izzy explained. "It says so here. About an hour and a half altogether, with an interval. And when you go to a concert or something, people always have a coffee in the interval, don't they? So we might have to organise that too."

"That's a lot," Maya said thoughtfully. "But I suppose people might not come for just, say, twenty minutes of clothes."

"Exactly. We can say it's a whole evening out." Izzy nodded. She looked really excited, Maya realised, and now she wasn't staring at her feet whenever she wanted to say something. Emily had stopped scowling at her all the time. She wasn't exactly being friendly to Izzy, but at least she wasn't muttering behind her back.

"How's your project going, girls?" Mr Finlay asked. "Ready to show me anything? Mrs Angel says you can go and see her tomorrow morning."

"Tomorrow!" Maya squeaked.

"Tomorrow's fine." Emily glared at her. "Please can we just have a bit longer to plan things before we show you? Even just ten minutes to make it all into a list?"

"All right. But I do need to see what's going on. I'll come back in ten minutes." Mr Finlay looked distinctly worried.

"He thinks we're going to get him into trouble with Mrs Angel," Maya whispered.

Poppy nodded. "We probably are! We were only supposed to be doing a project – a big poster or something. Like the others." She glanced around at the rest of the class. Most of the other tables had started making stuff to stick on to big wall displays.

Izzy laughed. "Not a fashion show, and a campaign to change all our school uniform. But we can make a display too – with all this stuff on it. Explaining how we came up with the ideas."

"What are we going to use for the rest of the time at the fashion show, though?" Emily asked, glancing round at Mr Finlay. "We need a plan before he comes back."

"What about your dance school?" Maya suggested. She'd seen Emily dancing in the Christmas play, and she knew she'd done loads of dance exams. "They do

shows, don't they? Would they do some dancing at a fashion show?"

Emily nodded slowly. "Most of the people in my ensemble group were in Year Six here last year. I bet they would. Katie Hodge, she's one of them. And Maria, and Ellie-May. And I can ask Miss Sara if any of the others can do it too."

Izzy was scribbling down notes. "Fashion show … clothes provided by Tara Nelson at Daisy… Models from Littlemoor Sixth Form College… Publicity by … us?"

The others nodded slowly. No one knew exactly how to go about doing publicity though.

"It can't be that hard," Maya said hopefully.

"OK. We need to use the stage blocks to make a catwalk. There's some shapes we can do here, look." Izzy riffled through her papers. "Mr Finlay always does the lights for the school play, doesn't he?" she added thoughtfully.

"And we need somewhere for people to change, it says here," Poppy pointed out. "The staffroom's behind the hall."

"What's the staffroom got to do with your project?" Mr Finlay sat down next to Poppy, and eyed them worriedly.

Izzy passed him the list, and Emily pulled out the petition she'd found, asking for Fairtrade uniform.

"Whoa. This is what you wanted to talk to Mrs Angel about?" Mr Finlay muttered, scanning through the list. "A fashion show... Fairtrade clothes, that's a brilliant idea. And the school uniform..."

"The cotton for our sweatshirts might be picked by children in Uzbekistan," Maya pointed out. "Lots of the cotton that's used in factories in India is. And we don't know where these are made." She held out her sleeve, looking at it worriedly. "We don't want to change the sweatshirts." She bit her lip suddenly, trying not to laugh, because Poppy was making a face. "We only want to find out if the people who make them could do a Fairtrade one. Or if we can get them from someone who does."

"Do you think Mrs Angel will let us?" Izzy asked anxiously.

Mr Finlay frowned. "I hope so. But this is all very ambitious, girls. Do you really think you can organise something like this?"

"We've already got the woman who runs the Fairtrade shop to say she'll provide the clothes," Maya explained. "And that would be the most difficult part, if we were asking lots of different shops for them.

So it's only the other bits. We don't know if Emily's dance school can be involved yet."

"Perhaps we could put up all the other Fairtrade displays for people to look at while they have coffee in the interval," Mr Finlay suggested. "Fairtrade coffee! And biscuits made out of Fairtrade ingredients!"

"Good one!" Emily sounded impressed. "Um, sorry…"

"I'm pretty sure she'll say yes to the fashion show, the sweatshirts might be more difficult." Mr Finlay frowned. "Of course, at the fashion show you could do a little presentation about it – get people to sign the petition."

"I found a video all about cotton picking in Uzbekistan, but I don't know how we'd show it." Maya looked hopefully at Mr Finlay. She knew he was good with things like that.

"Laptop and projector, Maya, no problem. You could have the whole presentation on the screen, with photos of the factories and things."

"Will you help?" Maya asked hopefully. "We wondered if you might be able to sort out lights."

Mr Finlay nodded. "Yes, if we're allowed to do it I'll definitely help – I should think Mrs Angel will say you need some staff involved anyway." He saw

Emily's disappointed face. "Don't worry. No one will take over your idea, girls. You'll still be in charge."

"I don't know if our uniforms are Fairtrade or not…" Mrs Angel murmured the next morning. Mr Finlay had left the rest of the class with Miss Grace, so he could explain to Mrs Angel that he would help too.

"I think they probably aren't, then," Maya said politely. "They'd make a thing of it, if they were Fairtrade, wouldn't they?"

Mrs Angel nodded. "Yes, of course." She smiled at Mr Finlay. "This wasn't what I was expecting when you told me your class were doing projects on Fairtrade."

Mr Finlay smiled proudly. "I know. They're thinking big."

"There is quite a lot that could go wrong, though." Mrs Angel looked down Izzy's list. "However. If you can sell enough tickets in advance to cover paying Mr Sampson to keep school open for the evening, you can have your show. Mr Finlay, can you go through the diary with Mrs Brooker, and find a good date? About three or four weeks away, perhaps."

"And we can do a presentation about Fairtrade

cotton, and ask people to sign the petition?" Emily asked hopefully.

Mrs Angel nodded. "That kind of thing has to be decided by the governors, though. Get lots of signatures and we'll see."

"Thanks, Mrs Angel!"

The girls hurried out of the office, and hugged each other in the corridor. Maya even felt like hugging Mr Finlay.

"I'll email Tara tonight and tell her we can do the show!" she said excitedly. "Then she can get her daughter started on finding models."

"Let's go and get a date set then." Mr Finlay went into the school office, and started explaining to Mrs Brooker, who was surprisingly enthusiastic.

"I've seen that lovely new shop," she told the girls, who were clustering round the door. "And this is the uniform catalogue. See if you can find anything about Fairtrade." She passed them a thick catalogue, marked with sticky notes here and there, and they leafed through it.

"It doesn't say anything about where the cotton comes from," Maya muttered. "Nothing about Fairtrade at all." She sighed. "So we'd have to find someone who could make jumpers with the school logo on."

"I'll put it on my list," Izzy said, and Maya laughed.

"You sound so organised! But I suppose we need to be." She gave a little shiver. She could hardly believe that Mrs Angel had said yes. Suddenly Izzy's list looked very scary.

"This is so exciting!" Tara sounded delighted. Maya had decided to phone the shop as soon as she got home from school, rather than emailing. "Tuesday the nineteenth. Just over three weeks. Right. I'll get Leah finding some models. But what about the girls' clothes, Maya? Will you and your friends model those? It would be nice, seeing as it was all your idea."

Maya gulped, feeling suddenly stupid. They hadn't even thought about that! Of course, if they were doing a show at school, all the girls would want to see the clothes for them too. "I'm not sure…" she faltered. "We might have to do back-stage stuff. But we can find people, definitely."

They agreed to meet up at the shop again on Saturday, and Maya put the phone down, feeling worried. Who should they ask? She loved the idea of modelling, but she had agreed to do the presentation about Fairtrade cotton with Poppy, and they were going to introduce the fashion show. Izzy was so organised she was going to be the show producer, and Emily was excellent at bossing people around, so she was being backstage manager, which as far as Maya could see was shoving everybody into the right place with all their stuff – something Emily was used to doing every day. Maya and Poppy were in charge of the publicity too. But the girls had all agreed that they'd help with everything. They'd told Mr Finlay he was the technical coordinator, and he'd pointed out that they ought to do a programme. It had gone on the List. It definitely had a capital L by now.

Maya jumped as the phone rang. She could hear Anna calling from downstairs that she was covered in pastry so please could Maya answer it.

"Hello?"

"Maya? It's me, Emily. I talked to Miss Sara after my ballet class, and she says yes, she's happy for us to dance at the fashion show, and she thinks the girls who do tap will come and do it too, because they've got a festival coming up, and it'd be good practice. And since she doesn't teach on Tuesdays, she'll come and help. But she says please can we put an ad for Sara's School of Dance in the programme."

"OK…" Maya frowned. She was beginning to

think that the programme ought to be more exciting that just a sheet of paper with everyone's names on it. Maybe she should get Poppy to draw a logo, or something. Poppy was the best at drawing in the class, everyone said so.

"Maya, do you think other people would give us things if we put in the programme that they had?" Emily asked her.

"Like what?"

"The coffee and stuff. If we asked a shop that sold Fairtrade coffee and tea and biscuits, and said we'd put a big thank-you in the programme?"

"It's worth asking, I suppose," Maya said doubtfully. She wasn't sure she'd be very good at that. She'd only been brave enough to ask Tara about the fashion show idea because it had all happened so fast.

"Do you think Izzy would write a letter?" Emily suggested hopefully. "She's clever at that sort of thing. She wrote all the stuff that convinced Mrs Angel." Emily's voice changed. "I'm saying she's useful, Maya, not that I like her."

"All right, all right." Maya shrugged. "I'm going to do the maths homework, and then I'll try and make something that looks like a programme. I guess that's a publicity job. And posters... Eek." Maya scribbled

on the back of her hand.

Designing the programme and the poster was actually a lot of fun – more fun than maths homework, anyway. Maya messed around with different fonts, and she had to leave a space for Poppy to draw something, but at least she had rough versions to show the others tomorrow.

"I hadn't thought about that." Izzy looked down at her list rather crossly, as though she thought it had let her down.

"I don't think I can be a model, not if I'm dancing and doing backstage too." Emily sighed.

"No, we'll all be too busy," Poppy agreed.

"So who are we going to get to do it?" Maya looked anxiously around at the others, squashed on to one of the playground benches. "It's got to be people who aren't going to go all giggly and stupid in the middle. And they have to turn up to rehearsals."

"Auditions," Emily said firmly. "It's the only way. Let's ask Mr Finlay. We can send a note to all the classes, for the afternoon register."

"I wish the bell would hurry up and ring!" Maya muttered.

Mr Finlay liked the idea of models from all

through the school, but he pointed out that they'd need parents to agree.

"How about I get Mrs Allwood to let you lot in the information technology room at lunch time? You can run up a letter to go home with all the girls tonight. The shop doesn't do boys' clothes, does it? Then you have your auditions tomorrow, and only people with a form saying they're definitely able to be there get to audition."

Emily nodded. "Otherwise people might just not turn up on the night."

Maya smiled hopefully at Mr Finlay. "If we're doing the letter, can we possibly use two computers, and do an invitation to the fashion show to go out too?" she pleaded. "Otherwise it's a bit sad to ask for models and not have people know what it's really for."

Mr Finlay rolled his eyes. "Yes. Now can we please do the register?"

"Right," Maya hissed to Poppy, as Mr Finlay moved names around on the whiteboard. "You've got till lunch time to design us a logo for the fashion show!"

Poppy whipped round, staring at her in horror. "What?" she whispered back.

"Ooh, good idea." Emily nodded approvingly. "Do you want to borrow my felt pens?"

"We'll make sure Miss Grace doesn't catch you," Maya promised.

Poppy huffed. "All right! What am I supposed to draw though? And it's numeracy, Maya, you'll have to fill in the sheet with your left hand so it looks more like my writing." She hid Emily's felt tips in her lap, and carefully tore a piece of paper out of the pad in her bag.

"Clothes?" Maya shrugged. "You know I'm useless at that sort of thing. Look, I did start on the poster and the programme – so you've got this space here for something to make them look really gorgeous." She beamed at Poppy. "And not too fancy, because it would be nice if it could go small on the ticket and the invitations."

"And it had better work in black and white as well as colour," Izzy pointed out. "I can't see Mrs Brooker letting us use the colour printer for anything more than the posters."

"Great," Poppy muttered, staring at the piece of paper dolefully. "That really helped…"

By lunchtime she had done it. Emily shot out of the

classroom to snag one of the coveted picnic tables at break, snarling so fiercely at a group of boys who wanted to swap football cards that they actually hurried away. The girls huddled round Poppy, who was muttering to herself and filling her pad with swirly designs.

"Oooohh! That one!" Maya said. "It looks good upside down, anyway." She was on the other side of the table from Poppy. "Are they birds?"

"No, it's an anteater," Poppy snapped. She was getting a bit frazzled. "Yes, of *course* they're birds." She turned it round to show Maya the design properly. Two little birds were flying off the page carrying a pair of jeans between them. "You like that one best?"

"Yes, it's lovely. The birds are cute, and the jeans look really cool."

Emily nodded. "I like it."

"Me too. Can you colour it in for the posters?" Izzy asked.

"Yes, but I'll copy it first," Poppy agreed. "Then I can go over bits to make the black-and-white one look clearer."

There was only one near miss, where Maya had to sweep a history worksheet over Poppy's drawing

very quickly, when Mr Finlay got it into his head to check their table. When the bell rang for lunch, they hurried off to the information technology room to scan everything in. Maya emailed it all to herself at home so she could put the designs on the poster and programme, and then she worked on the invitations with Poppy, while Emily and Izzy bickered in an almost-friendly sort of way about how to write the audition letter.

"How are you doing, girls?" Mrs Allwood came over to see. "That looks really lovely. You've only got a quarter of an hour of lunch left though – you need to go and eat something."

Maya checked her watch, frowning – surely it hadn't been that long? But Mrs Allwood was right. "I think the invitation's done. We just need to print them, and then cut them up – we put two on a sheet."

"I'll print them for you, while you go and eat. Perhaps you can cut them up this afternoon? Mr Finlay said you were having more project time."

"The letters are done, too. We've said the models need to be here by half-past six, so as to get made up and dressed in plenty of time," Izzy explained.

"And we put in a bit about not being allergic to make-up," Emily added smugly. "They always put that on the dance things."

Mr Finlay handed out the invitations and the audition letters at the end of school – a pile had gone to every class.

Maya and the others watched rather smugly as the rest of the class read the invitations, and commented to each other. None of the boys sounded very excited about it, but she supposed they shouldn't have expected that they would be. Nick Drayton made a snorting noise, and scrunched his invitation into a ball to throw it at Jensen, but Mr Finlay made him flatten it out and promise to hand-deliver it to his mother.

Ali and Lucy's table was buzzing. "A fashion show? Fairtrade? Like our project?"

Maya exchanged a delighted glance with Emily as she listened.

"And auditions tomorrow at lunchtime. Are you going to do it?" Lucy eyed Ali hopefully. None of Ali's clique would dare go along if Ali said she wasn't.

Ali shrugged. "Maybe. Not sure if I want to do some silly little show."

"As if she's an international catwalk model!" Emily hissed furiously.

Ali turned round and glared at them. "I suppose

you'll be auditioning, will you? And Izzy, of course!" She sniggered nastily, and Maya watched the red flush rise up Izzy's fair skin, from her neck upwards in a horrible wave. Maya put an arm round her, and even Emily moved protectively closer. She might not like Izzy much, but she disliked Ali a whole lot more.

"Izzy will definitely be at the auditions, Ali." Mr Finlay had come over without them noticing, and Ali looked slightly embarrassed – but only *very* slightly. "Seeing as she's the show producer, she'll be the one auditioning *you*."

SEVEN

"Her face…" Izzy purred. "It was brilliant…"

"I don't know whether we ought to hope Ali does come to the auditions or not," Emily mused. "She'd probably be quite a good model – she's so full of herself, she won't mind prancing down a catwalk. And it would be fun bossing her around. But she might try and take over."

"I reckon she'll have to come." Poppy was gathering her stuff together for after-school club. "If she doesn't, everyone will think she's scared."

"Scared of us?" Izzy asked blissfully.

Poppy grinned at her. "Yup. And she won't be able to take over, Emily, because if she starts being a pain, you and Izzy can just sack her."

"I love this fashion show." Izzy sighed.

"Oh, good, I'm glad I've caught you girls. Look, here are your posters." Mrs Brooker handed them a

sheaf of bright posters, and the girls admired them delightedly.

"You're so clever, Poppy," Maya said, stroking the glossy paper. "It looks great."

"Mr Finlay, can we put one up in here?" Emily asked.

Mr Finlay nodded. "But only one! You need to put the rest round school, and perhaps one at the library."

Emily nodded. "My mum's picking me up today, because Toby and James need new shoes again. She says we can go to Health Organics, that shop by the station, and ask if they'll donate us some Fairtrade coffee and tea and things. I know they have lots of Fairtrade stuff. They might put up a poster too. Mum reckoned a small shop might be better to ask than the supermarket, because we'd be able to talk to the owner."

"That's a good idea to save money." Mrs Brooker nodded approvingly. "I've worked out that you're going to need to sell at least twenty tickets before the event, so that we've got enough money to pay Mr Sampson for the extra hours, and cover the cost of printing the posters and programmes."

The girls looked at each other. Twenty wasn't all

110

that many, surely – but it was a bit scary.

"We haven't sold any yet," Maya said nervously. They'd put on the posters and letters that the tickets could be bought from the school office, or by emailing Mr Finlay. He'd said he didn't mind. "We haven't even printed any!"

Mrs Brooker laughed. "Actually, Mrs Allwood did them for you; she had a spare lesson this afternoon. And she's bought one, and so have I." She handed Maya a plastic wallet full of neat little tickets. "You girls had better keep these ones. If people order tickets by email, you'll have to give them out on the night. You've got thirty there. Mrs Allwood did a hundred and twenty altogether, that's as many as you're allowed in the school hall."

"Wow… Thanks, Mrs Brooker!"

Maya held the wallet, staring at the tickets excitedly. The show was really happening now!

But by Monday, with only two more weeks until the show, they'd only sold a few more tickets – not even enough to pay for the caretaker, and the printing.

It didn't help that someone was going round school scribbling on the posters. When Maya and Emily got off the bus that morning, they found Izzy and Poppy

standing by the one on the playground noticeboard. Izzy looked furious, and Poppy was drawing on the poster with some glittery pens.

"What are you doing?" Emily demanded. "Why are you drawing on it?"

"Was it you who drew on the one in the hall?" Maya asked them, sounding shocked. Someone had scrawled rude words all over it, and Mrs Angel had taken it down.

"Of course it wasn't!" Poppy shook her head. "I'm covering it up! If Mrs Angel sees what they've written on this one she'll have it taken down too, and we can't afford to print any more of them!"

"Oi! What are you doing?" Nick Drayton ran up to them, and pushed Poppy aside so he could see what she'd drawn on the poster. His mates Jensen and Charlie barged past the girls too.

"Watch who you're pushing!" Emily snapped. "And what's it to you what Poppy does, anyway?"

"She covered it up!" Charlie muttered, sounding disappointed.

"It was you!" Izzy hissed, glaring at them. "You wrote on our posters!"

"Didn't," Nick said automatically, but it was pretty obvious they had.

"Right. You owe us a pound." Izzy stuck her hand out.

"What?" Nick gaped at her.

Emily nodded. "Yeah, she's right. We'll have to get Mrs Brooker to print us two more posters now, and colour copies are fifty pence each, she told us."

"We're not giving you a pound!" Jensen snorted.

"So you want Mrs Brooker to invoice your mum for it then, do you?" Izzy asked him politely.

Jensen looked shifty. Maya thought he probably didn't know what invoice meant, and it was making him nervous.

"Because you've nicked a pound off the donation we're making to charity," Emily agreed. "So if you don't pay, your mum's going to have to."

"I've got fifty pence," Charlie muttered to Nick. "Mum gave it me for the Reception cake sale."

Grumbling, the boys scrabbled around in their pockets, and came up with ninety-eight pence, and a Mint Imperial. Emily and Izzy agreed to let them off the other two pence, and turned the mint down. The three of them wandered off moaning about how mean the girls were, and Emily and Izzy exchanged triumphant looks.

"Brilliant move with the invoice thing," Emily said.

"What does it mean?"

"Just asking for money." Izzy shrugged. "Dad sends out invoices for his gardening work. It just made it sound a bit more serious." She shook her head. "I can't believe they actually paid us!"

"I know. You two were amazing!" Maya hugged them both. "There's the bell. Let's go and see if Mr Finlay's sold any tickets over the weekend."

But when Mr Finlay arrived, the news wasn't good.

"No, I'm sorry girls, no one's emailed me yet. How's Mrs Brooker doing with the tickets?" Mr Finlay asked.

Izzy shook her head dolefully. "Hardly any. We need some more publicity."

Maya looked down at her feet, feeling miserable. She and Poppy had put up all the posters – lots of the local shops had agreed to have them – and she'd emailed and phoned the local paper, but no one had got back to her. They'd worked so hard – it would be awful if the event had to be cancelled. And almost worse if they did manage to sell twenty tickets. Twenty people rattling about in the school hall would be more than embarrassing.

"I'll try calling the paper again." She sighed. They'd done so much work – Poppy had made a brilliant presentation for their talk about Fairtrade, with lots of pictures. And Izzy had found two companies who would make sweatshirts like their school ones out of Fairtrade cotton. Emily had called them – she'd got her mum to let Toby and James have the sprinkler on in the garden, so there was no way they'd interrupt her while she was on the phone. They'd both agreed to send an information pack and a sweatshirt that the girls could put on display.

And they'd already auditioned all the models, and told them it was happening. Maya gritted her teeth. There was no way they were cancelling. "We have to sell more tickets," she muttered. "Just imagine what Ali's lot would say!"

Emily shuddered, and Izzy actually went even paler than usual, which was quite hard.

"My mum and dad are back today," Maya remembered. "And Anna hasn't got a ticket yet either. That's another three tickets."

Izzy nodded. "My aunt said she'd come. I'll tell her she has to ring Mrs Brooker. That'll get us to twenty, I think. But we need more, to raise money for building the school in Bangladesh. It's no good just not losing money. We have to actually make some."

"And how about the models?" asked Mr Finlay.

"Are you happy with them?"

Maya and the others exchanged glances. "I think so…" she said. "We've given all their sizes to Tara so she can choose outfits for them. And Tara's got some great models for the women's clothes from the sixth-form college. There's ten of them, and we've got ten as well. One of them's even from Reception!"

"And she was almost the best," Poppy giggled. "She's so cute, she was strutting up and down the hall!"

"Ali…?" Mr Finlay asked, raising his eyebrows.

Izzy sighed. "We had to let her. And Lucy, and Elspeth. They were good," she added glumly.

"The first rehearsal's at lunch time today," Maya told him. "Do you think it's OK if we chalk a catwalk on the hall floor? If we wipe it off afterwards? Mr Sampson says he'll put the stage blocks up for us on the day before the show, so we can have a rehearsal on them, but he can't keep taking them up and down."

Mr Finlay grinned. "I should think that bit of floor will be the cleanest it's ever been. I'm sure it'll be fine."

At lunch time the girls hurried over to the hall to arrange things before the rehearsal. For the real show, Mr Finlay would play the music they'd chosen over the proper speakers, but for today they'd agreed to use Maya's iPod – she had a little set of speakers that her dad had given her.

Emily had brought some chalk from home, and they put out chairs round the catwalk to give the feel of an audience.

"I thought there was going to be a *proper* catwalk." Ali stalked in, eyeing the chalk lines snottily.

"There will be on the night," Maya told her, resisting the urge to snap.

"It's hardly worth rehearsing, without a real catwalk," Lucy agreed, folding her arms, and scuffing at the chalk with her toe.

"Go away then. The rest of the models can just do another outfit each."

Maya, Poppy and Emily stared sideways at Izzy, trying not to look too shocked.

"Don't talk to me like that—" Ali started to say, but then the door banged as Miss Grace hurried in, followed by the other models. "Sorry I'm late, girls!" She noted Ali and Izzy facing up to each other, and frowned a little. "Is everything all right?"

"Is it?" Izzy snapped at Ali.

"Miss Grace, we haven't got a proper catwalk, it's really stupid…" Ali moaned.

"Of course you haven't, this is just a practice. Don't be silly, Ali. Right, Izzy, you're in charge, I'm only here to make sure no one falls off the imaginary catwalk." Miss Grace sat down in the audience, and beamed at Izzy.

Izzy held out her list in a slightly shaky hand. "OK. Emily's going to be in charge backstage on the night, and the running order goes like this – we start off with Poppy and Maya introducing the whole show, and explaining about Fairtrade clothes. They'll tell everyone about the campaign to have Fairtrade uniform right at the end, and then the fashion show starts. Lara, you come out first, wearing your school uniform, but with one of the new sweatshirts we're getting sent." Lara was the little girl from Reception. Both the companies had said they'd be sending a small sweatshirt. "And James will be with you – Emily's brother, you know?"

Lara looked a bit horrified, and so did Miss Grace.

"I've bribed him," Emily said hurriedly. "And he's only in this bit. We just need a boy to show the uniform off. If he doesn't mess up, he gets my week's sweets. None of the other boys wanted to do it. We did try…"

"So you have to remember to come in your school

dress on the night, OK?" Izzy reminded Lara. "And everybody else, we'll do you a list of anything you might need to bring. Hairbands and stuff. Different shoes. We'll give it to you at next week's rehearsal."

"Boring…" Lucy muttered to Ali, and Ali and Elspeth sighed loudly.

"Just put the music on," Emily muttered to Maya. "Then maybe they'll shut up."

Maya fiddled with the iPod, and set the music going. She just hoped they'd managed to get things to about the right length. They'd practised walking like models, and timed each other, and then picked all their favourite songs.

"OK, Lara and James first. Walk slowly down – smile! Twirl – and back up," Izzy yelled over the music.

Emily hovered at the other end of the catwalk with the list Tara had emailed them. When they met up at the shop at the weekend, she'd shown them the outfit ideas she was suggesting, although she still had to make the final choices, and add the accessories. "Ali and Elspeth in jeans next. Go! Oi, not you, Lucy…" She hauled Lucy back. "I'll *tell* you when to go!"

They went all through the running order, and

the girls' show ended with all the models posed at the end of the catwalk together (not James, as he'd refused to go on twice without double the sweets). Then the models from the sixth-form college would come on. Tara's daughter was rehearsing them at the college. They were all going to pose again together at the very end, but rehearsing that would have to wait.

"How did it look?" Izzy asked Maya and Poppy anxiously.

"Brilliant – except we've still got two songs left from the girls' bit. Either they need to walk slower, or we'd better cut some out."

"I wouldn't cut any," Emily called. "They've got to change, remember. I bet there might be some places where we're slow going on."

"When do we get to see the clothes?" Lucy asked.

"Not until the day before," Maya told her. "Tara, from the shop, she's going to bring them for the rehearsal after school on the Monday. We'll check everything fits, and you can practise changing. That's going to be in the staffroom, and Mrs Angel says we can have the display screens to go between the staff room and the end of the catwalk, like a backstage area. That all gets set up on Monday afternoon, and then Tuesday afternoon there's the final rehearsal.

Oh, and don't forget to buy tickets," Maya reminded them.

"But we get free tickets, don't we?" Ali demanded.

"You don't need a ticket, you're in it," Maya pointed out.

"For our parents!" Ali snapped back. "Performers get free tickets."

"No." Maya rolled her eyes sideways at Emily and Poppy and Izzy, in a "help me!" look.

"Since when?" Emily asked. "We don't for school plays. And this is for charity. You need to buy tickets."

Ali heaved a massive sigh. "I don't know why I'm bothering," she muttered. But it was obvious she wasn't going to walk out. She'd enjoyed prancing down the catwalk too much.

"We really need to sell some more tickets," Emily muttered, as they walked back to the classroom to bolt down their lunch before the end of the break.

"I know. I'm doing my best," Maya said apologetically.

"It's just going to look so stupid with hardly anyone there!" Emily scowled.

"Emily! I can't exactly drag people off the street, you know!"

"Hey, calm down." Poppy put a hand on Maya's arm.

"*She* can calm down! I'm doing my best." Maya felt like crying. They were all working so hard – she had been up till eleven last night, working on the presentation, after she'd told Anna she was going to bed. Why did Emily have to have a go at her?

"Well, maybe that's just not good enough!" Emily snapped. "I've had two extra rehearsals for the dance group this week. I was finishing my homework on the bus this morning."

"I know you were, I told you all the answers!" Maya cried furiously.

Emily humphed, but it was true. "If it was in the paper, we'd have sold lots of tickets," she muttered accusingly.

"I emailed them twice, and I phoned," Maya hissed. "What am I supposed to do?"

"She's doing her best," Izzy began, but Maya was feeling so upset now that Izzy didn't really sound as though she meant it.

"Fine," she spat. "You do it! This was my idea in the first place, don't you think I want it to work?" She stormed off back to the classroom, but she didn't bother getting her lunch, just stashed her iPod in her locker, and shot out to the corridor, barging past Emily and the others coming in. Then she hid in the girls' loos until the end of lunch, trying to cry without making herself look like she had. It hadn't worked very well, she realised gloomily, as the bell went and she checked herself in the mirror on the way back to class.

Emily, Poppy and Izzy were huddled up muttering to each other as she walked in. Poppy smiled at her worriedly, and tried to say something, but Maya didn't feel like smiling back. She stalked in, and sat down as far round the table from them as she could. And she didn't talk to them all afternoon, ignoring the whispers and mutterings she could hear from the other side of the table.

Maya wasn't sure what she was actually going to do, and an afternoon of science didn't really help her decide. Was she walking out on the fashion show? She didn't want to. It had been her idea in the first place! But if the others thought she wasn't doing her bit, she certainly wasn't going to beg them to let her back into the gang.

I won't... she thought to herself angrily, as she marched out to get on the bus. *Why should I?* But she could feel the anger slipping away already.

She wished she hadn't lost her temper with Emily so easily. It was because she was tired, and worried too, and Emily had just made her feel worse.

Emily didn't sit with her on the bus – of course she didn't. Maya watched her walk up the aisle and hesitate for just a second, but then she flounced past and sat on her own. Maya spent the whole journey home with her nose pressed against the window so that no one could see she was crying again.

She opened the front door, and slung her bag on to the floor wearily. Then she realised that the hallway was full of luggage. Of course! Mum and Dad were home!

She'd only just made the connection when her mum hurtled out of the kitchen and hugged her. It was so nice that Maya started crying all over again.

"Maya! What's the matter, sweetie?" Her mum held her at arms' length, looking at her worriedly. "Did you miss us?"

"No … I mean, yes. But that's not why I'm crying," Maya sniffed.

"Tell me." Her mum sat down on the stairs, and pulled Maya down next to her.

Maya sighed. There was such a lot to explain. She'd spoken to her mum on Skype a few times, and texted her, but she hadn't told her about the fashion show. Maya wasn't sure why, although their calls had always been pretty short because Mum was working. Dad had started thinking about some new lyrics while he was out there, and Maya got the feeling he wasn't listening that hard when they'd talked. And she'd wanted to save it as a surprise. Some surprise. Large tears ran down her nose.

"The project – remember we talked about it?"

"Fairtrade?"

"Uh-huh. We're doing a fashion show, at school. Two weeks from now, on Tuesday night."

"A fashion show?" Her mum sounded confused. "But … how?"

"I asked Tara, from the Daisy shop, if she'd do it with us. We went to see what it was like, and I thought of the show while we were there. We're raising money to help build a school in Bangladesh."

"But Maya, that's amazing!"

Maya sighed. "It is, isn't it? Except I've messed it all up. No one's coming. We've just about sold enough tickets to pay the caretaker to open up the school, but the hall's going to be almost empty. It'll look so stupid. Ali and the others will never let us forget it, and Emily and Poppy and Izzy hate me!"

"OK, slow down." Her mum was frowning. "Forget Ali, I can't stand that girl and I've never even met her. Why do Emily and the others hate you?"

"I'm in charge of publicity. Me and Poppy, but Poppy drew the poster and everything. I'm supposed to get us in the paper, and they won't email me back."

"Typical," her mum muttered. "Local papers are always like that. But that's not your fault, Maya."

"Emily had a go at me about it. She sort of said it was…"

"How sort of?" Her mum hugged her tighter.

"I suppose I went off on one a bit…" Maya admitted. "But she was being mean. She does that, though…"

"Uh-huh. But you still like her."

Maya's bag beeped, and she reached down to grab her phone, frowning at the strange number.

borrowed mum's phone 2 say sorry. will u sit with me tmrw? E xxx

Maya laughed, feeling suddenly shaky with relief. Emily didn't hate her after all.

"Is that from Emily?"

"She says she's sorry." Maya leaned against her

mum's shoulder. She was so tired her bones felt wobbly. "I'll text her back in a minute." She keyed the message in, her fingers shaking a bit from relief.

ok. sorry I lost it. M xxx

"That doesn't actually solve your problem, though," her mum said thoughtfully.

"You really know how to cheer me up…" Maya whispered. But it was true. Even if she and Emily were friends again, they still had an awful lot of tickets to sell.

"You know I said I'd love to help with your project?" her mum asked quietly.

"Mmm?"

"Well, there is one way we could get some publicity pretty easily."

Maya blinked at her. And then she realised what her mum was talking about. India Kell just had to say that she was supporting their little fashion show, and it would definitely get in the local paper. It would probably be on the front page.

"Oh… Would you do that?"

"Of course I would, if you want me to. I'd love to, Maya, I think it's brilliant, what you're doing. It

would be such a shame if more people didn't get to hear about it." She was silent for a minute. "But it's just what you didn't want."

Maya nodded. "I know. It wasn't going to work for much longer, though. I hate not being able to talk about you to my friends. And I really want to be able to have them round."

"They're good enough friends that you don't mind them knowing, then?"

"I think so. Even Izzy, and I've only really known her a couple of weeks." Maya slumped forward, leaning her chin on her arms. "It isn't just them, though. It would mean everybody knows."

Her mum sighed. "I know. But it's your friends that matter, Maya. The important thing is that you know your friends won't change when you tell them the truth."

Maya sniffed. "We might sell out of tickets," she muttered.

"If you don't, I'll be having words with my agent. So… Yes? I can go and phone her office now if you like. Get a publicist on to it."

"OK." Maya sat up slowly. "I'd better tell the others tomorrow."

EIGHT

Emily climbed on to the bus looking a bit nervous, and she hesitated next to Maya's seat, as if she wasn't sure it was OK to sit down.

Maya patted it. "Come on."

"So you're still talking to me, then?" Emily muttered.

"If you're talking to me…"

"I was being really unfair. I sort of knew it anyway, and then Poppy called me last night. She said you'd been doing loads of work, and I shouldn't have gone on at you. Anyway, I'm really sorry. And I know it was all your idea. You can't give up on it, Maya, it's special."

"I know. I don't want to. I think I've sorted out the problem with the tickets, too." Maya smiled, and then sighed.

"How?" Emily asked excitedly. "Did you get an

129

answer out of the local paper? Are they going to put it in?"

"Yeah. Kind of. Do you mind if I wait till we get to school and tell you all in one go? It's a bit difficult to explain."

Emily nodded slowly, and there was an uncomfortable silence for a couple of minutes. "How's the dancing going?" Maya asked at last.

"It's good," Emily muttered. "Lily and Maisie, you know, the twins in Year Five? They do a ballet duet together, they said did we want them to do it at the show. I said probably. Was that all right?"

"Sounds good to me." Maya twirled her hair round her fingers nervously. She really hoped her friends weren't going to be too weird about her news. She felt odd chatting with Emily the rest of the way to school – they both seemed to be trying too hard, and there were great big gaps, and then they'd both try to talk at once. It was as though they'd forgotten how to talk to each other properly.

They hurried off the bus, and Maya hated feeling relieved.

"So, do you want to find Poppy and Izzy then?" Emily asked uncomfortably.

"Mm. Sorry, Emily. I know I'm being weird."

Emily shrugged, but Maya suspected her feelings were hurt, and she sighed miserably. This was going to be a disaster.

"You're talking to each other then?" Poppy asked, smiling with relief, as she and Izzy saw them coming.

"Um, yes." *Or trying to, anyway,* Maya added silently to herself.

"Maya wants to tell us all something," Emily muttered. She was obviously trying not to sound grumpy, and Maya grinned at her gratefully.

Maya perched on the railings outside the main door, and looked round at the others, all staring at her. "I think I've sorted the publicity out. I mean, we're going to get lots of it."

"Really? That's amazing!" Poppy beamed at her. "How?"

Maya was silent for a moment, eyeing her shoes. Eventually she dragged her eyes up again. "My mum got her agent to call the paper. And the local TV news as well."

"Her *agent*?" Emily repeated.

"Well, her publicist, I think."

"What's that?" Poppy whispered to Emily, but not quietly enough.

"It's someone who makes sure Mum's in the news

enough. And for the right things."

"Is your mum an actress?" Izzy asked, frowning.

Poppy nodded as she finally understood. "Is this why you never talk about her?"

"Sort of. But she's not actually an actress, she's a singer." Maya took a deep breath. "She doesn't use my dad's name, and I do, so her surname isn't Knight like me. She's India Kell."

All three of them stared at her.

"You might not have heard of her," Maya added uncertainly. "She's a singer…"

"Of course we've heard of her!" Emily snapped. "Your mum's India Kell? Really? Maya, if you're having us on, I'm going to kill you."

"I'm not. Look." Maya had thought of this, and she'd taken a photo on her phone that morning, of her and her mum in the kitchen.

"Wow… That really is her. And you…" Poppy murmured.

"Why didn't you say?" Emily did sound hurt, Maya realised, which was just what she'd been worried about. She took a deep breath.

"Because that's why I left my old school. I had one really brilliant friend, Macey – and I'm going to get her to come to the show – but all the others, they went

132

on and on about my mum the whole time. It was like *she* was the thing that mattered, not what I was like at all. I got really sick of it, and I begged Mum and Dad to let me move, so I could just be me."

"You've been lying to us all this time." Emily sounded indignant, but also intrigued.

"I tried not to. But it was horrible, not being able to have you all over to my house. Especially after you invited me to yours, Poppy. I felt really mean."

Emily giggled. "We just thought you had a deep, dark secret. Like me. Except Toby and James and Sukie aren't that secret, unfortunately…"

"Well, I sort of did," Maya agreed.

"What did your mum's … publicist say to the paper?" Izzy asked. "And did you really mean it about the TV news?"

"Uh-huh. She told them that Mum was supporting a Fairtrade fashion show, organised by children at a local school. She didn't exactly say it was because I was doing it, but they'll probably work it out. They were really keen, they said they'd put something in this week's paper to say it's happening, and then a big article afterwards too. Oh and Cara, she's the publicist, she called Mum this morning and said she was working on getting it on the radio as well. That

would be good, because they'd advertise it on the day, I think. The TV news won't be much good for getting people to come."

"Yeah, we should tell them we're not interested." Emily giggled.

Izzy snorted with laughter, and then Poppy and Maya caught it too. They couldn't stop laughing, even when the bell went. They were sitting waiting for Mr Finlay to do the register, sniggering every so often. If they stopped, it only took Emily muttering, "Not interested," and they all started off again.

Mr Finlay looked at them a couple of times, and Miss Grace was definitely glaring, but they couldn't help themselves.

"That table over there needs to – yes, Mrs Brooker?" Mr Finlay glanced up as the classroom door opened, and the school secretary hurried in. She looked quite flustered, and she kept glancing over at Maya and the others.

"What have we done?" Poppy murmured.

"*Maya?*" Emily nudged her.

"Ummm… It might be something to do with Mum." Maya shrugged. "I don't know."

"Maya, Emily, Poppy and Izzy, can you go with Mrs Brooker, please?" Mr Finlay called. "And try and make it quick, girls!" But he was grinning.

"Mrs Brooker, what's happening?" Maya called after her, as she hurried back down the corridor.

"I've got a man from the local paper in the office, and I've already had someone from the radio, and the BBC on the phone. What have you girls been *doing*?"

"Can I go and brush my hair?" Poppy wailed. "Does he want to take photos?"

Emily sighed. "It would be the day I've got this dress on, it's way too tight. Oh well."

"You all look lovely. Come on, he says he's got to go and see a giant fish afterwards or something, so he's in a hurry. I've already called all your parents to ask if you can be in the paper. Well, not yours, Maya, obviously."

Maya was about to ask why not, when they got to the office and she saw her mum leaning against the wall by the door, chatting to the man from the paper. Maya saw her smile at a girl Maya knew from Year Four. She'd obviously arrived late, and was waiting for Mrs Brooker to sign her in. The girl was standing in reception staring at Maya's mum, her mouth open in astonishment, as though she wasn't sure she was real.

"Oh, Olivia, you had a doctor's appointment, didn't you? Go on into your class then." Mrs Brooker shooed her down the corridor.

"Look who that is!" Olivia muttered to Maya and the others as she went past, and she turned back about six times before she reluctantly disappeared round the corner.

Maya's mum looked at her daughter uncertainly, as if she wasn't sure she was allowed to say anything.

"Hey, Mum." Maya smiled at her.

The man from the paper glanced from Maya to her mum and back again, and muttered, "Wow." And then, "I didn't realise your daughter was at this school."

"We've been keeping it quiet, for Maya's sake," her mum explained. "But when she and her friends came up with the fashion-show idea, and their Fairtrade uniform campaign, we decided to make use of some publicity, since it's such an amazing cause. They were having trouble getting a response from your paper," she added, very sweetly.

"Oh … really?" He looked slightly embarrassed. "We *are* very busy."

"So where would you like to take the photos?" Maya's mum asked helpfully. "Perhaps in front of the poster for the show?"

The photographer nodded – Maya had a feeling he was just doing what he was told now – and posed them round the poster. He did have a go at suggesting one of just Maya and her mum, but stopped when he got glared at.

"And now you'd like the girls to tell you about the show," Maya's mum told him firmly, and Maya tried not to laugh. She didn't see her mum in full superstar mode very often – it was amazing the way people just nodded and did as she said.

"We can email it to you if you like," Maya suggested. "All the details."

"Er, yes. Thanks."

"I'm really sorry," Maya's mum told Mrs Brooker, when he'd gone. "I thought they'd arranged it all with you, when they asked if I'd come over here. I didn't realise he was just turning up!"

"Oh, it doesn't matter." Mrs Brooker looked more flustered than ever, and Maya realised that her mum made the school secretary nervous. She smiled secretively at her feet. Mrs Brooker was usually so scary – it was funny seeing her in a flap.

They had caught the local paper on just the right day

– it came out a couple of days later, on the Friday.

"Just ready for everyone to read it over the weekend, and ring up for their tickets on Monday morning," Izzy said happily. She'd got her dad to stop at the newsagents that morning, and she'd brought two copies to school. She and Poppy had raced over to Maya and Emily, waving them at their friends as they got off the school bus.

"Did they get all the details right?" Maya asked anxiously. They were on the front page, which was great, but it was no good if they'd put the wrong date, or anything like that.

"No, it's all fine, I checked," Izzy said. "And they put in about it all being in aid of building a school in Bangladesh." She giggled. "Actually I think they nicked some of it straight from what you wrote, Maya."

"Not this bit," Maya muttered, reading what the article said about her and her mum. *Maya Knight, 10, shares her mother's famous looks, with waist-length red hair.* "I'm cutting it off…" *Maya and her friends are also campaigning for Park Road School to change to a Fairtrade school uniform, after a school project helped them to discover the shocking truth behind many of the items we wear.* "Ooh, they must have rung up Mr Finlay," Maya muttered.

138

MAYA'S SECRET

The girls' teacher, Paul Finlay, told The Post, *'The class were shocked by the images of child workers. It's great that the project has given them such enthusiasm for helping children like themselves.'"*

"No one's said anything to you about it?" Maya asked Poppy and Izzy uncomfortably. "About – you know – my mum?"

"No. But I think Ali's seen it. She keeps looking at you." Poppy moved closer to Maya, protectively. "She does *not* look happy."

"I haven't done anything to her…" Maya murmured, glancing behind her. Poppy was right. Ali was glaring at them.

"You know what she's like, she can take offence at anything," Emily said, shaking her head.

Maya, Izzy and Poppy looked at her meaningfully, and Emily scowled. "What? I'm not that bad. Not as bad as Ali, come on! That's so unfair!" She went pink, and added, "OK. Sorry."

Maya hugged her. "You can have a go at Ali when she storms over here and accuses me of making it all up. I bet she will."

Actually, she waited until they were in class. By that time the news had spread around, and quite a few people were gathered around Maya, asking about

her mum and why she hadn't told anyone before.

"It's really sad when people are so boring they have to go on and on about their parents," Ali said loudly, and Maya sighed.

Emily was just about to start telling Ali where to get off when Nick Drayton, of all people, waded in instead. "Shut up, Ali. You're just jealous. If you had a famous mum, we'd never hear the end of it. Maya, do you think your mum would sign an autograph for my mum? Your mum's her favourite singer, she's got all her CDs."

"Ooh, and mine!" Loads more people were asking now, and Ali sat down, seething.

"Maya's mum's coming to the fashion show." Izzy had her business head on. "If your mum comes too, Maya's mum could sign her CDs."

"And she'll do photos. But you'd better tell your mum to get a ticket quick, they've almost sold out," Maya added.

"You liar!" Emily whispered admiringly, as Mr Finlay yelled at everyone to sit down, and half the class muttered to each other about making their mums buy tickets at the end of school.

"I know, but it's nearly true." Maya smiled. "They *will* be almost sold out."

140

"It's just marketing," Izzy said approvingly. "But you realise if we sell out, that means a hundred and twenty people coming to watch this show."

Maya swallowed. "Ye-es. Maybe we'd better have a production meeting at break, do you think?"

"Wow." Maya walked further into the hall and looked around. "It looks…"

"Exactly the same as it always does, except with something that could just about be a catwalk if you look at it sideways on a good day?" Emily asked.

"Um, yeah."

"I know. It isn't exactly rock and roll, is it?"

Mr Finlay had given the girls the Monday afternoon out of class, so they could get the hall ready for the first rehearsal with all the models after school that evening. The stage blocks were in place – and Izzy had made a note on the List to give Mr Sampson some Fairtrade chocolate to say thank you – but otherwise, it looked (and smelled) like the place where they had PE. And assembly. And rainy lunchtimes. It wasn't inspiring.

"It'll look better with the lights dimmed," Izzy said, trying to sound hopeful. "Mr Finlay's going to put spotlights on the catwalk, remember."

"It just looks a bit boring, though," Poppy sighed. "We need a backdrop, or something."

"A what?" Maya asked her.

"Like a wall decoration. And something cool to go over those screens." Poppy nodded at the blue display screens that Mr Sampson had set up across the back of the hall, covering the staffroom door so there was a backstage area.

"Hang on. Can't we use the back wall as the screen for the projector?" Izzy asked. "Usually it's the other way round, because we sit that way for assembly, but there's no reason it couldn't go on to the wall. And then we can have Poppy's poster design as a backdrop, when there's nothing else on the screen."

"That would definitely cheer it up," Maya agreed. "Poppy…"

Poppy eyed her warily. "What?"

"Could you paint something to go over those screens? Some more things like the little birds?"

"By tomorrow?" Poppy asked.

"Yes."

Poppy sighed. "I'm just going to ask Mr Lucas in the art room if he's got any dust sheets. Or something." She grinned. "Have fun moving a hundred and twenty chairs!"

Even though they'd teased Izzy about the List, Maya was grateful for it by the time all the models arrived after school. Izzy was just so organised. She'd also bullied her dad – who wasn't all that keen on watching a fashion show – into being in charge of refreshments. Emily's hunch had been right, and the Health Organics shop had donated Fairtrade tea and coffee and sugar in exchange for a big mention in the programme. Poppy's mum was making six batches of biscuits at that very moment, and they'd used some of the ticket money to buy her the Fairtrade ingredients.

But the List wasn't much help for dealing with a load of eighteen-year-olds, who were wandering around the hall, going, "Aaaawww! They're all so little! Aren't they cute?" And, "I wonder if Mrs Angel still goes on about polishing shoes," and lots of other stupid stuff, instead of listening to Izzy, who was trying to get everyone's attention and answer about six questions at the same time.

In the end Emily got fed up, and jumped on to the catwalk. "Oi! Can you all listen, please!" she yelled at the top of her voice, and for once, everyone did. Even Ali and Lucy, who'd been standing over Poppy and making rude comments about her painting. If

they didn't watch it, Maya reckoned she was about thirty seconds away from painting their shoes.

"Tara will be here with the clothes in a minute, and she's going to put them on rails in the staffroom," said Izzy. There was a chorus of *oohs* at this, as everyone, even the eighteen-year-olds, realised they were going to get to go into the staffroom. "They're all labelled, and you've got to make sure everything goes back on the right hanger! Miss Grace is going to help with that, and she'll be there tomorrow to help you do quick changes as well."

Maya beamed gratefully at Miss Grace. She was being a total star.

"Anything else?" Emily hissed at Izzy.

"Mr Finlay's just trying out the lights and the music, and as soon as Tara gets here, we'll get started. Oh, you can't leave any stuff in here – it's all got to go in the staffroom, like it will tomorrow."

"She's coming!" Maya rushed over to open the doors for Tara and Leah, who were dragging two huge rails of clothes.

"Everyone find a spot to change in the staffroom!" Emily yelled, after Izzy had whispered in her ear.

"It looks amazing," Maya whispered, half an hour later. "Ooops, where's the next two?" Then she giggled as Ali shot out on to the catwalk, having obviously just been shoved on in a hurry by Emily. Ali turned round and glared at her, and stomped down the catwalk looking a lot less model-like than usual. Lucy, who was meant to be with her, just didn't turn up at all. Izzy made a note on her glitches page, tutting.

But it did look good, even with the mistakes, Maya agreed. The lights and the backdrop made a huge difference, and the clothes looked gorgeous.

"Let's just hope it goes as well tomorrow," Izzy muttered, as all the models posed together at the very end. "Fingers crossed."

"That's a TV camera!" Emily squeaked. "I didn't really believe we'd be on TV!"

A reporter in a very smart purple suit was chatting to Maya's mum, and Maya tucked her hands behind her back to stop herself nibbling her nails. She was so nervous. The hall was filling up already, and Mrs Brooker, who'd agreed to come and take the tickets, had told her that she'd actually had to turn some people away. They'd stuck big SOLD OUT labels over the posters, but obviously people had hoped they'd be able to blag their way in.

"I wish I hadn't said we'd do this presentation," she muttered to Poppy.

Poppy hugged her. "You'll be fine. I brought some of my herb tea, do you want some? It's very good for nerves."

Maya laughed, and felt a bit better. "No, thanks. I'll be OK."

"Are you two ready? It's nearly seven," Mr Finlay reminded them.

Maya swallowed, and nodded. It definitely wouldn't have been a good idea to have the tea – she felt like she might throw up.

They were doing their bit from the side of the catwalk, so they didn't have to come on from the staffroom, just hurry up the steps. They hovered close by, and then the main hall lights went down, and the backdrop changed from the *Welcome to Our Fairtrade Fashion Show!* slide, to one saying *What's Fairtrade All About?*

Maya could see her mum and dad standing at the side of the hall – no seats left, then! Her mum blew her a kiss. Maya tried to think of all those full chairs as money for building the school, instead of people staring at her, and started to talk.

Afterwards, she was never quite sure if they actually

did all of their presentation. It certainly didn't seem to take very long, and there were bits she was sure she didn't remember saying. Still, people clapped a lot, and at least it was done. She scrambled down the steps and waited anxiously next to Izzy at the edge of the hall as the music began, while Emily scowled at her little brother and whispered something in his ear that could well have been a death threat.

But he and Lara walked down the catwalk beautifully, and the audience purred at them. Maya could hear it – "Oh, aren't they sweet!"

"It's going so well," Izzy whispered, her eyes glittering excitedly in a flash of the stage lights. "Everyone's on time, even. And that's the last of the girls – now they just have to all come back on."

Maya nodded, and sighed with relief as the whole group paraded back down. Only the older girls to go now.

They were about halfway through when someone tapped her shoulder. "Maya! Come on! You too, Izzy."

"What is it?" Maya's heart thumped painfully. What had gone wrong?

"A surprise. Come on, you have to go round the back." Maya's mum hurried them behind the

screens in the dark, and quickly stuffed them into the staffroom, which was full of people scuffling around for clothes and cursing in whispers as buttons wouldn't do up and lipstick got smudged. Miss Grace and Tara were racing around like mad things, sorting everybody out.

"We've just got time, hurry up!" Tara pushed a pile of clothes into Maya's arms. "Get changed!"

"What?"

Her mum smiled at her. "Maya, you've got to go on – all of you! This was all your idea. Tara's picked out amazing clothes for you all. Emily's already wearing hers, I told her beforehand, she couldn't have stopped to change now. Hurry up, you've only got about two minutes!"

Maya pulled on the little purple flowery dress – it looked good with her silver flip-flops, luckily – and let Tara push some pink flowery clips into her hair.

The rest of the models were pouring out on to the catwalk now, all the girls from school, too, for the end of the show.

Mr Finlay turned the music down a little, and announced, "Now a huge thank you to the organisers of tonight's fashion show – Maya, Emily, Izzy and Poppy! And our special guest, India Kell!"

Maya's mum grabbed Maya and Emily and pulled them up the steps on to the catwalk.

Maya blinked at the lights. Everyone was clapping! And she could see a red light on the TV camera – they were filming this bit.

"Wave!" Poppy muttered, and Maya did as she was told. She really couldn't believe they'd organised all this. And it had worked!

Her mum hugged her at the end of the catwalk, and the others too. "I'm so, so proud of you," she whispered in Maya's ear, and Maya nodded, and smiled up at her gratefully.

"Me too…"

The dance part of the evening after the interval had gone really well, even though Emily had been so buzzed by the success of the fashion show that she very nearly danced off the edge of the catwalk.

"It's not the same shape as a stage, that's all!" she muttered, when Maya asked her afterwards if she was OK. "I'm fine! Katie once did a pirouette and slipped right into the front row, at least I didn't do that."

"The man from the local paper took loads of photos of you," Izzy told her encouragingly. "Not

the bit where you – er – wobbled, don't worry!"

Emily sniggered, forgetting about her near-fall. "I love your mum, Maya. Didn't you see, that reporter was going to leave at the interval, but she wouldn't let him, she kept steering him about and making him talk to people, and then your dad actually stood in front of the doors to the hall with his arms folded, he looked like he was proper security, and the man didn't dare walk out!"

Maya grinned at her. This was what she'd been worried about – everyone at school finding out who her mum was and telling her how much they loved India Kell. But not because she was so scary people wouldn't dare leave halfway through a fashion show… Then her face flattened, and the others turned to see what she was looking at.

Izzy took a deep breath, and Maya nudged her encouragingly. "Remember you're still in charge!" she hissed, as Ali and Lucy and Elspeth walked up to them. But Ali's dad was following, Maya noticed. And he looked surprisingly nice and normal for someone whose daughter was so mean.

"You're the girls who organised all this, aren't you," he boomed cheerfully. "Fantastic effort! Great idea! Ali's been so excited about it – she's hardly talked about anything else for the last fortnight. This lot just wanted to say thanks for letting them be involved before I take them home."

"Really?" Maya asked, smiling sweetly at Ali.

"Mmm." Ali went pink, and muttered something that might have been "Thanks" before all three of them scuttled away.

"Now I can die happy…" Emily said, gazing blissfully after her.

"Me too." Maya nodded.

"We ought to go and help your dad wash up all the coffee stuff, Izzy," Poppy sighed. "But there's a secret leftover biscuit stash," she added, brightening up. "I hid one of Mum's tins."

"Excellent, I'm starved." Maya flung an arm round Poppy's shoulders. "If I wash up, will you feed me biscuits?"

The friends laughed and headed off to help with the clearing up. It had been a brilliant night!

♡

"Good morning, everyone!" Mrs Angel looked around the packed school hall during assembly the next day and smiled. "I hope everyone who attended had an enjoyable time at the fashion show last night."

Maya looked sideways at her friends. They'd all

gone as pink as she had, and Izzy let out a nervous giggle.

Their head teacher continued. "I thought it was excellent! I want to thank Maya, Izzy, Emily and Poppy for all their hard work and for teaching us so much about such an important subject. And I'd like the recipe for your delicious biscuits, girls! We haven't counted all the money you raised yet, but I thought you'd like to know that I spoke to the head of the governors earlier and I've got some good news. After such a fantastic effort, we have decided that the school should do its bit for fair-trade. So we'll try our best to source the school uniform ethically from now on."

Everyone cheered loudly, and Maya hugged Poppy, and then Izzy and Emily too. "We did it!" she whispered. "I can't believe we actually made Mrs Angel do something!"

Mrs Angel raised her hands for silence. "I will let you know how we get on. But for now, I think everyone deserves a big round of applause, don't you?"

As the four friends walked back along the main corridor to their classroom, chatting delightedly, a splintering crash echoed somewhere round the corner. Mrs Angel's voice rang out behind them.

"Toby! James! Come here right now!"

Emily groaned and tried to hide her face in her sweater. Maya laughed. "Do you think we could convince Mrs Angel to let us have sweatshirts with hoods? Then you can disappear every time your brothers get into trouble."

Emily sighed. "It's worth a try. I never thought school would listen when we started all this, and look what we've managed!" She grinned. "We need to use our powers for good, Maya. I vote that now we campaign for a fair-trade chocolate machine in the playground…"

Like funny books? You'll LOVE these!